Aeschylus

Prometheus Unbound

With Introd. and Notes by A.O. Prickard

Aeschylus

Prometheus Unbound
With Introd. and Notes by A.O. Prickard

ISBN/EAN: 9783744781954

Printed in Europe, USA, Canada, Australia, Japan

Cover: Foto ©Andreas Hilbeck / pixelio.de

More available books at **www.hansebooks.com**

Clarendon Press Series

AESCHYLUS

PROMETHEUS BOUND

WITH INTRODUCTION AND NOTES

BY

A. O. PRICKARD, M.A.

FELLOW AND TUTOR OF NEW COLLEGE

SECOND EDITION, REVISED

Oxford

AT THE CLARENDON PRESS

1883

London

HENRY FROWDE

OXFORD UNIVERSITY PRESS WAREHOUSE

7 PATERNOSTER ROW

PREFACE.

THE text of this edition is, with the exceptions noticed in the Appendix, that of Dindorf's Second Edition (Oxford, 1851). Where this has not been followed, the change has almost always been made in favour of a reading which has manuscript authority as against one which rests on conjecture. Entire consistency can scarcely be looked for in such a process: the general aim has been to combine the practical advantages of a familiar text with the greater respect to Aeschylean MSS. which scholars now allow to be their due. In one noteworthy passage (l. 49), where Dindorf gives the reading of the MSS., a time-honoured conjecture has been admitted. Several of the variations will be found in Dindorf's last text (1869); but it has been thought better to make his earlier one (which is substantially that of the older 'Poetae Scenici,' etc.) the basis of that now published.

In the notes the editor has wished to give all necessary explanation of the text as printed—

σιγῶν θ' ὅπου δεῖ, καὶ λέγων τὰ καίρια.

They are intended for those who read this play at an early stage of their study of Greek. As far as possible, all controverted matter, of text or of interpretation, has been avoided. Happily the play is one in which this can be done with comparative impunity : still the ungracious-ness has often been felt of giving 'a silent vote' where the views of eminent scholars are divided. But it is to be remembered that, in the case of a writer so straight-forward as Aeschylus, only one view of his meaning can be right; therefore the choice of some one must at last be made, either by the editor, or by the reader; all other views go for nothing, so far as the interpretation of the author, the first duty of both editor and reader, is concerned.

References to other plays and other authors have been very sparingly given ; to passages in the play itself more copiously. It has been said that ' Aeschylus will generally be found his own best interpreter,' and the truth of this may be abundantly seen, even within the compass of one short play. A careful reading of almost any part of Homer will suggest valuable illustrations of the language and thoughts of Aeschylus.

It is perhaps unnecessary to acknowledge assistance throughout derived from Mr. Linwood's Lexicon to Aeschylus, and Mr. Paley's editions. Liddell and Scott's Lexicon is specially rich in information about this play, and should be constantly at hand. For some of the matter of the Introduction the editor is indebted to Professor Westphal's most interesting essay on the Prometheus Trilogy.

August 1, 1878.

INTRODUCTION.

WHEN Chaos came to an end, the first rulers of the Universe were Earth and Heaven. Earth bore many children; among whom were Ocean, and the Titans, and the Cyclopes, and the Giants, such as Cottus, and Briareus, and Gyes. But one of her sons, Cronus, rose up against his parents, and seized the throne for himself. He did not enjoy it long unpunished; for Zeus, his son, overthrew him, and became lord, the third in succession. But before he was seated firmly on his throne he had a great battle to fight with the Titans, which lasted ten years, and ended in the complete victory of Zeus. The Titans were sent down to the lower darkness, as Cronus had been before them; and Zeus established his rule firmly, allotting to the other Gods, whom with him we call the Olympians, their several offices.

At the time of this conflict we first hear of Prometheus. He was son of Iapetus, a Titan, and Atlas was his brother. But he is sometimes spoken of as though he were himself a son of Earth and a Titan. Endowed with foresight to read the future, he counselled his kinsmen, the Titans, not to come to a trial of strength with Zeus, but to make the best terms they could with the conqueror who was to be. They would not listen to him, but scorned his politic advice. Then he saw nothing left for him but to stand by Zeus, and the defeat and punishment of the Titans was in large part due to him.

Zeus was not in these early days of his power the beneficent ruler of whom we read in Homer, 'the father of Gods and men.' No sooner was his victory secured, than he displayed all the insolence of an usurper, to whom authority is a new thing; drawing all the reins of power into his own hands, recognising no law but his own will, and trusting no one but himself. If this was his behaviour towards the Gods who were his kin, men came off far worse. Miserable and brutish as their state was, he would take no heed of them ; but was even ready to sweep away their whole race. But Prometheus withstood the tyrant to his face, for he saw that men were capable of better things. And first he stole fire, which Zeus had expressly refused them, carrying it down in a hollow reed from heaven. With this he taught them many arts, which could not be practised without fire. He taught them also to count, number being the key to all sciences ; and gave them the faculty of memory; and he showed them how to break, horses for use, and to sail the sea in ships, and to cure diseases, and to read dreams. But above all he gave them Hope, that they should not be always looking forward to death, but, buoyed up by hope, might endure the life of the present.

This interference between the tyrant and his creatures was more than Zeus could brook. He sent his messengers to seize Prometheus and bind him fast in a rocky gully in Scythia, or, as most say, to a crag in the Caucasus ; there, till Zeus should be pleased to loose him, to expiate his great offence. Further he sent an eagle, or vulture, to visit him from time to time, and torture him by preying upon his liver. But Prometheus, strong in the righteousness of his purpose, and in his full knowledge of all that was before him, and moreover knowing that he possessed a secret which, though not till after many hundred years of agony, would enable him to dictate his own terms to Zeus, would not lower his tone ; but scorned the threats, and turned a deaf ear to the overtures, of the ruler of Olympus.

Such is the story set before us by Aeschylus in the 'Prometheus Bound,' and almost every detail given above can be supplied from that play; which is so arranged that no spectator, however uninformed, could fail, if he listened attentively, to catch the drift.

But the story, as it came into the hands of Aeschylus in older poems which we can still read for ourselves, such as those of Hesiod, contained many other incidents. Some of these Aeschylus passed by, as being good enough allegory, but little to the purpose of the great main drama, or action, which he had chosen to set forth. Such, for instance, was the account of the brother Epimetheus ; who was wise after the event, as Prometheus, whose name signified 'fore-thought,' was wise before it. Others were simply childish ; as the tale that, in apportioning the flesh of an ox, Prometheus had played a trick upon Zeus, and so raised his anger. And these could be of no use in a play addressed to the highest feelings of an Athenian audience.

The part of the story actually comprised in the 'Prometheus Bound' is very small. It is confined to the exhibition of Prometheus being bound to his rock by the agents of Zeus, and afterwards discoursing to certain persons who in succession visit him there. The play ends, as its second scene (if we may use the word) begins, with a defiant appeal to the powers of Nature to witness the tyranny of Zeus ; which is then visibly made manifest in a mighty convulsion of the elements, overwhelming, but not overawing, the chained Immortal. In one sense the action does advance ; for, through what falls from Prometheus, we see our way forward to a solution in the far future ; but nothing passes before the senses of the spectator which makes any change in the dramatic situation itself.

Let us ask what special points of interest we are likely to find in such a drama.

In the first place, we have a display of human action presented to us on a great scale. Though the persons who take part in it are Gods, and Titans, and Nymphs, yet they all act, and feel, and think, as men and women. Just as Aeschylus himself and the other tragedians chose from the materials found in the epic poets such stories of royal houses as they felt to be suitable to their art—those for instance of Thebes and Mycenae—in order that they might show their countrymen life like that of Athenian men and women, but magnified and ennobled ; so here, in the loves and strifes of these superhuman beings, Aeschylus intends us to see character as truly human as is that of Satan or of Abdiel in our great English epic. The story of Prometheus was not made the subject of a drama by either

Sophocles or Euripides, though the former is said to have treated it incidentally; it is a theme eminently well suited to Aeschylus ; and, had this play been only known to us by name, we could to a great extent judge how immense would have been our loss.

Passing from the story itself to its treatment by the poet, it is clear, from what was said above, that we are not to expect the interest to be artificially sustained, as in the 'Oedipus Tyrannus,' by an elaborate plot. There is no series of incidents by which the fortunes of the hero pass from the height of good to the depth of bad fortune ; still less is there, as in the play just named, that ingenious arrangement (known to Greek critics as περιπέτεια) by which the real tendency of the action is masked, so that what seems to be making for the hero's happiness is in reality contributing to his downfall. Nor is there any room for those brilliant surprises, as effective on the ancient as on the modern stage, by which an apparent stranger is shown to be a person of first-rate importance to the plot, and its course entirely changed by the discovery (ἀναγνώρισις). What we are to look for is firstly _suffering_; so real as to appeal straight to our deepest feelings, but so grand as to chasten and subdue their outburst. And, secondly, _character_. Few plots could be better devised for the exhibition of character than one in which a many-sided hero like Prometheus, his nature stirred to its depths by injustice done to himself and to others, is brought into contact successively with persons so varied as are the remaining actors in the drama. This will be seen most clearly by an examination of the play itself. We must add two other points of attraction, which many at least of the audience must have found in it. One was the weird and supernatural element which pervaded the piece ; the strangeness of the mountain scenery, the presence of gods and nymphs on the stage, the aerial cars of Ocean and his daughters, the appearance of Io. The other is to be found in the account of regions lying on the limits of the habitable world, known as yet dimly and by legend, but which the adventurous spirit of travellers like Herodotus was soon to win for the domain of geographical knowledge. Lastly, though the plot itself is, as we said, extremely simple, it has all the interest of a well-told tale ; the prophecies of Prometheus being cunningly elicited from him, broken off when the interest is thoroughly awakened, and resumed at the right moment, according to the example set by Homer in that best of stories, the Odyssey.

The several Acts of the play correspond to the 'parts' into which Greek plays were technically divided by ancient critics, so far as that division can be properly applied to plays so early as those of Aeschylus. It will therefore be convenient to take these parts in order.

I. Πρόλογος : (all that part of the play which precedes the entrance of the Chorus, ll. 1–127).

The play opens in the mountains of Scythia. Aeschylus has not here, as in one at least of his lost plays, followed the usual story, which described Prometheus as chained to a crag in the Caucasus, identified by later legend with Kazbek, one of the highest peaks of that range. A ravine, or gully, occupies the centre of the view shown to the audience ; and in it Prometheus, represented by a huge wooden effigy, is placed. Three other figures are seen ; those of Strength and Force, two demons, sons of Styx, never far, Hesiod tells us, from the presence of Zeus ; and that of Hephaestus, who is their unwilling companion. Only one of the demons speaks ; and he gives his orders to the god with the utmost harshness and insolence. Hephaestus' patience is sorely tried, but he must needs obey the orders. The unwelcome task at last over, he calls on his companion to come away, which, with a last scoff at the prisoner, now firmly secured, the other consents to do. In this scene the physical details are brought plainly before the audience. The ringing strokes of the god's hammer are heard far over sea and land, the stake is visibly driven through the middle of the body. Probably the superhuman size of the effigy and its palpably wooden construction went far to make the representation tolerable even in an Athenian theatre.

We have now had the situation presented to us in a sin-

gularly bold and effective opening. No one of the audience
can fail to understand where and how the action is pro-
ceeding. Moreover, from the way in which Hephaestus is
treated, we are prepared to find how oppressive and un-
constitutional is the new despot of Olympus. Hephaestus
is himself an Olympian God ; mild and good-humoured in
disposition, he is in Homer the butt as well as the crafts-
man of the other Gods, and he stands in wholesome awe
of the power of Zeus.

As soon as his tormentors have departed Prometheus
breaks silence. In a dignified appeal to the powers of
Nature, in the midst of which he hangs ; the air rushing
swiftly past him, the mountain-sources of great rivers,
the distant rippling sea, Mother Earth beneath his feet,
the Sun, whose eye sees all ; he calls upon them to witness how greatly and how unrighteously he suffers. Then
the thought of his own full knowledge of the future and
of his real greatness of purpose arises to stay any pas-
sionate thoughts, and to nerve him to bear the bitter
present.

II. Πάροδος and First ἐπεισόδιον, ll. 128–396.

As he ponders on these things he becomes aware of some
new presence ; it draws nearer, and the air is audibly beaten
by wings, while a faint sea smell heralds his visitors, the
daughters of Ocean, who form the Chorus. They have
heard afar in their deep sea-caves the noise of the hammering, and have come forth, drawn by curiosity and by fear,
laying aside their maidenly reserve, and even coming out
without their sandals. We are left to picture to ourselves
how—

'Afar, like a dawn in the midnight,
Rose from their seaweed chamber the choir of the mystical sea-
maids.'

Aeschylus only shows us how they arrive wafted by wings
through the air, from which they at last (l. 279), in compliance with Prometheus' earnest request, alight. These
are no conventional Chorus, to offer prudent advice, and to
draw moral conclusions ; but are real persons, consistent with

themselves, and as beautifully conceived as are Nausicaa and her handmaids. Maidenly and modest, full of womanly curiosity and womanly pity, most happy when there is something practical to be done, with the simplest conceptions of duty and piety, yet unshaken in their resolve to stand by their injured friend at whatever cost to themselves, they admirably relieve the sternness of the play. And in dealing with minds so eager to sympathise, yet so little able to sound the depths of his purpose, the gentler side of Prometheus' nature comes clearly out. Nothing can exceed the courtesy and respect with which he treats them, answering or parrying their questions with all good-humour, asking pardon for his silence, and mediating, as we see him do, with Io, to secure them the pleasure of hearing her story from her own lips.

There is, strictly speaking, no πάροδος (entrance-song), the Chorus at once beginning a lyric dialogue with Prometheus, their part in which falls into strophe and antistrophe. The ἐπεισόδιον, or Act, which is thus begun, is in two parts.

(a) In the preliminary dialogue, ll. 128–276, the Chorus assure Prometheus that their hearts are with him, and speak in unexpectedly severe terms of the iron rule of Zeus, Prometheus drops some hints as to the secret which will one day put Zeus into his power ; but the Chorus receive these rather as the proud words of an injured spirit than as being really prophetic. In answer to their questions, he proceeds to tell them the whole story of his offence against Zeus, allowing that it was deliberate, and only complaining that the punishment was disproportionate and capricious. Finally, he invites them to descend to earth, and listen to what more he has to tell them. They obey, leave their aerial station, and arrange themselves in the ' Orchestra ' in front of him, ready to be attentive listeners.

(b) But the narrative is broken off by the entrance of a new person. This is Ocean, the father of the Ocean nymphs ; who arrives in a car drawn by a griffin, or some fanciful winged beast. He is one of the gods of the old order, a son of Earth, who has been reconciled to Zeus,

and has found it possible to live on the terms dictated by
the conqueror. He has heard with sincere regret of his
kinsman's trouble, and comes to offer sympathy and advice,
enforcing the latter with many an old saw, and many a
word of caution. The pride of Prometheus is deeply hurt
both by the sympathy and by the advice ; he answers with
extreme dryness to the platitudes of Ocean, expressing
wonder that he should have thought it worth while to leave
his streams and caves to come and see so sorry a spectacle,
and charging him, as he valued his own safety, not to inter-
vene in the contest, even as mediator. Ocean, who has
come to give good advice, and does not relish listening to
it, at last gets somewhat hot ; but he is really zealous to
serve his friend, and it is only on a suggestion from Prometheus that any attempt to mediate may but serve to in-
crease the present punishment, that he offers to go. He
now remembers that his griffin must be impatient to get
home to his own stable ; and so in his odd equipage the
old god starts off, and leaves Prometheus and the Chorus
alone together once more.

(During the visit of Ocean his daughters have nòt spoken.
They had with difficulty obtained his consent to their own
absence from home, and perhaps were not very anxious to
be seen by him. But as they have been standing in the
Orchestra while his car has been hovering over head, they
have not met his eye. Now that he is gone, they break into
a short song (the First στάσιμον), mourning for the fall of the
grand old system of Cronus and his peers, and for the fate
of Prometheus, which is bewailed by men in every land, as
is that of his brother Atlas by sea and the depth beneath it.)

III. Second ἐπεισόδιον—lines 436–525.

Prometheus now speaks, not to continue the promised
account of his future sufferings, but to ask pardon for his
silence, caused by pondering on the. ingratitude of Gods.
On that he will not dwell, but tells his hearers at full length
of all the good things of which he was the author for men.
To a well-meant, but ill-grounded, remark of the Chorus, that
surely one who has so mightily helped others will one day
hold his head higher than Zeus, he answers mysteriously—

he will indeed one day be freed, but it will be by the inter-
vention of Necessity, which Fate, not Zeus, directs. Pressed
to say how this is to be, or how anything can be in store for
Zeus save to reign for ever, he declines : this is his secret,
and the present is not the time for it to be revealed.

(The Chorus, in an Ode of Sophoclean sweetness (the
Second στάσιμον), pray that they may never, on their part,
thus cross the path of Zeus, nor fail in their simple duties,
nor offend in their words ; but may live in bright innocence,
linking day to day by hope and joy. How sad Prometheus'
case ! how differently was it with him on the day when he
led Hesione home, his bride, and the Ocean nymphs joined
in the marriage-hymn !)

IV. Third ἐπεισόδιον—lines 561–886.

This simple prayer of the nymphs brings them into
strange contrast with the person who now appears, and
whose presence causes an interruption to the plot during
the whole of this division of the play. Io, daughter of Inachus, king of Argos, was, while yet in her father's house,
vexed by nightly visions, which told her that she was be-
loved of Zeus. Her father sought an interpretation from
many oracles ; and was at last plainly told to set her out of
his house, that she might be a wanderer on the face of the
earth. With a heavy heart he obeyed ; and instantly, by
the jealous wrath of Hera, her form was turned into that of
a heifer ; and the herdsman Argus, with myriad eyes looking every way, was set to drive her from land to land. When
he was killed by Hermes, a fresh plague succeeded, the
gad-fly, which torments cattle ; and so the poor maiden had
no rest. She has now reached the desolate region where
Prometheus is chained ; and appears suddenly, with her
strange, unnatural figure and gait, upon the stage. While
she is uttering a wild cry of pain, she becomes aware that
she is in the presence of another sufferer, and implores him
to tell her whither she has been led. He addresses her by
name, and his words show that he knows all her story.
Wondering at this, she asks to know who he is, and recog-
nises the friend of mankind. Then she begs to be told what
he can tell her about her own future wanderings. He con-

sents, though with hesitation, for he knows how painful the account will be. But the Chorus interpose ; they do not know Io's past history, and so the prophecy will have little interest to them. So at the request of Prometheus, who wishes at once to gratify the Chorus, and to let Io have the relief of pouring her troubles into friendly ears, she tells her sad, strange story. The Chorus are shocked and distressed ; but it is at their request that Prometheus traces Io's future wanderings over seas and through many lands, adding that what he has now told her is but the beginning, the first wave of a very sea of woe. Io's anguish on hearing this leads to a short dialogue, from which we learn her connection with the general plot. First, she, like Prometheus, is a victim of the tyranny of Zeus, and has equal reason with him to wish that the hated reign were over. Secondly, it is one of Io's own descendants who shall hereafter deliver Prometheus. So the prophecy of the last Act (l. 513) is continued in fuller detail. Prometheus now bids Io choose whether she will hear what remains about her own future, or the name of his deliverer. But the Chorus, with girlish confidence, again interpose. ' Both boons,' they cry, 'one for her, one for us !' The two stories really make but one. Prometheus brings Io's wanderings to an end in the city Canopus at Nile's mouth. There Zeus shall restore her reason ; he shall but touch her with soothing hand, and she shall bear a son, who shall be named Epaphus. Of his race shall come Danaus, the father of fifty daughters. These (of whom we read more in Aeschylus' play, ' The Suppliants') shall murder each her husband, each save one—

> ' Una de multis face nuptiali
> Digna '—

She shall bear a kingly line at Argos, and of it shall come the deliverer ; who is not here named, but whom we know to be Heracles, or Hercules, son of Alcmena. He shall be a famous archer ; and, as we know by what has reached us of another play, shall shoot the eagle, Prometheus' loathly foe. All has now been heard ; with a wild cry and gesture Io bounds away, and is seen no more.

The bearing of this remarkable Act upon the plot has been already pointed out. We should further notice that its introduction enables the poet to bring Prometheus into contact with a new type of character, and to elicit his prophecy in a striking and dramatic manner. Still it has very much the character of what is called in Epic poems 'an episode,' and was probably introduced into the play partly, at least, for the sake of variety, and in order to gratify that growing interest in the geography of distant countries to which reference has already been made. The details of Io's course present a good many difficulties, some account of which will be found in the notes.

(The Chorus, in the Third στάσιμον, shortly lament for Io's sorrows, and pray that they may themselves ever be spared the ills of an unequal marriage.)

V. ἔξοδος, or closing Act (line 907-end).

Prometheus protests that Zeus, great though he be, and firmly seated though he seem, shall yet come to an end ; and that in that day his silly artillery of bolt and flame shall avail him nothing. So let him do his worst, for his time is short. The Chorus, interposing with words of caution, do but awaken a more defiant mood. But his proud words have reached the ears of Zeus ; whose lackey, as Prometheus styles Hermes, arrives, and bids him reveal his secret about the marriage which is to imperil Zeus. Neither threats nor persuasion alter the sufferer's determination to disclose nothing. As well try to talk over a wave of the sea, as look for bended knee and upturned hands from him. Hermes does his part faithfully, and shows all the adroitness of speech attributed to the Messenger of the Gods, but in vain. Finally he displays his threats ; the earthquake, the fall of the mountain to bury its prisoner, the eagle to prey upon his vitals ; and declares that there shall be no respite until some God become a substitute, going down of his own free will to Tartarus. One gentle word of advice from the Chorus, a fresh assertion from Prometheus that he knows all and will endure all, a warning to the Chorus, which they indignantly reject, to stand aside, a second warning that they will only have themselves to thank for the trouble which will be their portion ; and the end comes : earthquake, dust-storm, jagged lightning, whirlwind. ' O majesty of Earth, my Mother ! O air rolling around for all the universal light, thou dost see how unrighteously I suffer !'

Every one who has read the ' Prometheus Bound' will at once ask the question, to what solution does the poet point, and what reconciliation is possible between two such antago-nists as Zeus and Prometheus ? Let us see how far the play itself helps us to answer this question. And first we must observe that nearly all which we are told about the future comes from Prometheus' own lips. He is throughout the expounder of prophetic lore to listeners who, with the excep-tion of Hermes, know nothing but what they see. Briefly the conditions of his deliverance are these :—

1. He possesses a secret about a marriage to be one day projected between Zeus and a mortal, the issue of which, if it take place, shall be a son stronger than his father, who shall seize the throne for himself. This danger can only be averted from Zeus by Prometheus giving him timely warn-ing, so that he may avoid making such a marriage.

2. He will not reveal this secret before he is released.

3. Zeus will not release him or be reconciled to him until an immortal consent to go down to Tartarus in his place.

4. He shall be released by a descendant of Io in the thirteenth generation, a great archer.

With greater or less certainty we may read the interpre-tation as follows :—

Hercules, the descendant of Io in the required degree, shoots the eagle and releases Prometheus, by whom he is hailed as ' dearest son of a most hated father.' Now a substitute is found in the person of Chiron ; who, being sick of an incurable wound, is weary of his immortality, and gladly consents to die. Zeus is thus free to be reconciled with Prometheus, and the latter is free to tell his secret. The marriage which endangers Zeus is one which he wished to make with Thetis ; being warned, he betroths her to a mortal, Peleus, and she becomes the mother of Achilles.

We know that Aeschylus wrote two other plays on this story; and it is probable that the three were a ' Trilogy,' that is, a series of three tragedies forming a continuous whole, and followed by a Satyric play, in which some ludicrous incident of the story was sometimes set forth. If this was so, we cannot doubt that the Prometheus Unbound (λυόμενος) immediately followed the extant play. We know that the Chorus in it were Titans, and that it contained the same abundance of geographical detail which we have in the story of Io. With regard to the Prometheus Firebearer (πυρφόρος) there is more doubt. It is often assumed that it stood first of the three, and contained the story of the theft of the fire. As however there hardly seems to be room for any such preface to our play, which is perfectly intelligible without any, it is more probable that it really stood third, and contained the final reconciliation scene, in which Prometheus appeared

> 'Extenuata gerens veteris vestigia poenae,
> Quam quondam silici restrictus membra catena,
> Persolvit pendens e verticibus praeruptis';

and a glorification of him as the giver of fire to men. Those who know the conclusion of the 'Eumenides' will have no difficulty in imagining how such a reconciliation may have been presented. (See also Soph. O. C. 55.)

It is clear then that such a conclusion to the story as is given in the 'Prometheus Unbound' of our own poet Shelley, involving the total overthrow of Zeus, is widely (as it is intentionally) different from that given by Aeschylus. But how did Aeschylus, who in all his other plays speaks with genuine reverence of Zeus, allow himself here to draw a picture in which the King of the Gods is shown as a selfish, suspicious, cruel tyrant, the character of all others most repulsive to an Athenian mind? Perhaps no complete answer can be given; but we will suggest a few considerations, some of which have been already stated.

(1.) The great interest of the play is that of human character. The mythological bearings are pushed aside, and even the religious interest for the time overshadowed, by the great conflict of will between Zeus and Prometheus. The story of the rebellion was not invented by Aeschylus; only he has chosen to breathe into the forms of older poets the spirit of human life. Aeschylus thought of Prometheus as Milton thought of Satan, not as a mere rebel to be crushed, but as a living will and mind to be realised and pourtrayed.

(2.) Our play contains only a portion of the story. In the sequel the poet had the opportunity of representing Zeus as grand, benevolent, and generous, having learnt much by length of rule, and having passed from a tyrant into the wearer of a time-honoured crown ; and, coming last, this side of the picture would leave the deepest impression.

(3.) In the Prometheus Bound we hear of the tyranny of Zeus chiefly from those who suffer from it. Neither Zeus himself, nor any of the greater Olympian Gods, appear upon the stage ; and it is open to us to suppose that his tyranny may have been even necessary in the age of general violence from which it had just emerged.

(4.) Perhaps something further is intended. Aeschylus may have wished to paint one of those situations in which the difficulty of all human action is seen. The poet himself and every generous heart in the audience felt that Prometheus was right ; that they could wish nothing better for themselves than to act, in his case, as he had acted. And yet he was also wrong ; where the fault lay it would be hard to say, whether in his over-eagerness, or in his self-reliance, or in his pride ; but somewhere or other there is that in his case which makes it impossible to say that he was unreservedly right, and Zeus unreservedly wrong. The 'Antigone' of Sophocles affords the best example of a plot constructed with such a purpose ; and Bishop Thirlwall's remarks on it (Essay on the Irony of Sophocles) will explain fully what is here only indicated.

Thus it may perhaps be true that the key-note of the Prometheus Bound, or rather of the whole Prometheus Trilogy, is to be found in the line of Hesiod,

ὡς οὐκ ἔστι Διὸς κλήπτειν νόον οὔτε παρελθεῖν,

or in the beautiful words of the Chorus, 'Never shall the devices of mortal men overpass the great harmony which Zeus ordains.'

We have no evidence as to date, except the reference (in
l. 367) to an eruption of Aetna which perhaps occurred in
B.C. 479. But other considerations would also lead us to
assign it to at least as late a part of the literary life of
Aeschylus, which lasted from about B.C. 500 till his death
in B.C. 456. Though the plot is not elaborate, the play is
thoroughly mature work ; more mature, it would seem, than
any of his other compositions, except that Trilogy which we
know to have been his last. The versification is smooth.
The third actor is not required ; on the other hand, in the
scenes where Io or Hermes is present, the Chorus is so
really an actor, that the advantage of having three persons
present at once, an arrangement by which Sophocles gains
so much in the complex development of character, is in effect
obtained. The choric songs are much shorter than in the
other plays of Aeschylus ; and this, if we have received them
as originally written, would point to the play being a late
one. But, whatever its date be, the work seems to be
both mature and finished. The Latin critic Quintilian tells
us that Aeschylus' plays were so rough that they were al-
lowed to be represented in a more finished form after his
death, and that many poets received crowns for such re-
production. If we allow the general justice of the criticism,
we must claim an exception for the 'Prometheus Bound.'
Were it in our power to beg such a favour from Aeschylus,
most of us would be sorry to ask him to reconstruct the
play, or to re-write a single scene of it. And a modern poet
or play-wright, who should take such a task upon himself,
would hardly earn a crown of gold or of bay.

The style of Aeschylus is naturally straightforward.
When he is difficult, the cause lies in the difficulty which
he himself found in making the words which were at
his command express the lofty thoughts and imagery
which poured into his mind. He had not learned the
secret, as Sophocles, both by observation of the merits
and defects of his predecessor, and by close study of
language itself, afterwards did, of writing genuine poetry
in language apparently simple and little differing from
that of prose. He formed his style, partly by study of

the poems of Homer, partly by venturing himself to form new words, like his contemporary Pindar, who 'per audaces nova dithyrambos Verba devolvit.' To some of his compounds attention has been called in the notes, as showing special 'boldness,' because the author uses them in a sense of his own, and not in that which, according to analogy, they ought to bear. His metaphors are characteristic, showing great vigour of thought, and much observation of men and things. They are drawn from the experiences of the soldier and of the sailor, from animals wild and domestic, and from all the habits and occupations of men. A particular type of metaphor common in Aeschylus is noticed on l. 880. The constructions are usually simple ; like all bold writers, the poet sometimes finishes a sentence on a somewhat different model from that on which he began it, but he never deliberately blends two constructions for the sake of effect. The versification has much freedom and impetuosity, caused in great part by the use of the long words mentioned above, and by the caesura often coming in the fourth foot of the Iambic verse (Hephthemimeral caesura). In some of his plays there is great disregard of caesura, which gives an appearance of roughness to the verse. This will not be found to be the case in the 'Prometheus.'

Some topics of interest, connected with this play, such as the origin and development of the myth of Prometheus, and the early relations of Greece and Egypt, as indicated by the story of Io, are not here discussed ; because they do not bear directly upon the purpose of the poet himself, which it must be the first object of all his readers to understand.

ΠΡΟΜΗΘΕΥΣ ΔΕΣΜΩΤΗΣ.

B

ΤΑ ΤΟΥ ΔΡΑΜΑΤΟΣ ΠΡΟΣΩΠΑ.

ΚΡΑΤΟΣ ΚΑΙ ΒΙΑ.

ΗΦΑΙΣΤΟΣ.

ΠΡΟΜΗΘΕΥΣ.

ΧΟΡΟΣ ΩΚΕΑΝΙΔΩΝ ΝΥΜΦΩΝ.

ΩΚΕΑΝΟΣ.

ΙΩ Η ΙΝΑΧΟΥ.

ΕΡΜΗΣ.

ΠΡΟΜΗΘΕΥΣ ΔΕΣΜΩΤΗΣ.

ΚΡΑΤΟΣ.

Χθονὸς μὲν ἐς τηλουρὸν ἥκομεν πέδον,
Σκύθην ἐς οἷμον, ἄβατον εἰς ἐρημίαν.
Ἥφαιστε, σοὶ δὲ χρὴ μέλειν ἐπιστολὰς
ἅς σοι πατὴρ ἐφεῖτο, τόνδε πρὸς πέτραις
ὑψηλοκρήμνοις τὸν λεωργὸν ὀχμάσαι   5
ἀδαμαντίνων δεσμῶν ἐν ἀρρήκτοις πέδαις.
τὸ σὸν γὰρ ἄνθος, παντέχνου πυρὸς σέλας,
θνητοῖσι κλέψας ὤπασεν· τοιᾶσδέ τοι
ἁμαρτίας σφὲ δεῖ θεοῖς δοῦναι δίκην,
ὡς ἂν διδαχθῇ τὴν Διὸς τυραννίδα   10
στέργειν, φιλανθρώπου δὲ παύεσθαι τρόπου.

ΗΦΑΙΣΤΟΣ.

Κράτος Βία τε, σφῷν μὲν ἐντολὴ Διὸς
ἔχει τέλος δὴ κοὐδὲν ἐμποδὼν ἔτι·
ἐγὼ δ' ἄτολμός εἰμι συγγενῆ θεὸν
δῆσαι βίᾳ φάραγγι πρὸς δυσχειμέρῳ.   15
πάντως δ' ἀνάγκη τῶνδέ μοι τόλμαν σχεθεῖν·
ἐξωριάζειν γὰρ πατρὸς λόγους βαρύ.
τῆς ὀρθοβούλου Θέμιδος αἰπυμῆτα παῖ,
ἄκοντά σ' ἄκων δυσλύτοις χαλκεύμασι
προσπασσαλεύσω τῷδ' ἀπανθρώπῳ πάγῳ,   20
ἵν' οὔτε φωνὴν οὔτε του μορφὴν βροτῶν

B 2

ὄψει, σταθευτὸς δ' ἡλίου φοίβῃ φλογὶ
χροιᾶς ἀμείψεις ἄνθος· ἀσμένῳ δέ σοι
ἡ ποικιλείμων νὺξ ἀποκρύψει φάος,
πάχνην θ' ἑῴαν ἥλιος σκεδᾷ πάλιν·   25
ἀεὶ δὲ τοῦ παρόντος ἀχθηδὼν κακοῦ
τρύσει σ'· ὁ λωφήσων γὰρ οὐ πέφυκέ πω.
τοιαῦτ' ἐπηύρου τοῦ φιλανθρώπου τρόπου.
θεὸς θεῶν γὰρ οὐχ ὑποπτήσσων χόλον
βροτοῖσι τιμὰς ὤπασας πέρα δίκης.   30
ἀνθ' ὧν ἀτερπῆ τήνδε φρουρήσεις πέτραν,
ὀρθοστάδην, ἄυπνος, οὐ κάμπτων γόνυ·
πολλοὺς δ' ὀδυρμοὺς καὶ γόους ἀνωφελεῖς
+ φθέγξει· Διὸς γὰρ δυσπαραίτητοι φρένες·
ἅπας δὲ τραχὺς ὅστις ἂν νέον κρατῇ.   35
ΚΡ. εἶεν, τί μέλλεις καὶ κατοικτίζει μάτην;
     τί τὸν θεοῖς ἔχθιστον οὐ στυγεῖς θεόν;
     [ὅστις τὸ σὸν θνητοῖσι προὔδωκεν γέρας.]
ΗΦ. τὸ ξυγγενές τοι δεινὸν ἥ θ' ὁμιλία.
ΚΡ. ξύμφημ', ἀνηκουστεῖν δὲ τῶν πατρὸς λόγων   40
     οἷόν τε πῶς; οὐ τοῦτο δειμαίνεις πλέον;
ΗΦ. ἀεί γε δὴ νηλὴς σὺ καὶ θράσους πλέως.
ΚΡ. ἄκος γὰρ οὐδὲν τόνδε θρηνεῖσθαι· σὺ δὲ
     τὰ μηδὲν ὠφελοῦντα μὴ πόνει μάτην.
ΗΦ. ὦ πολλὰ μισηθεῖσα χειρωναξία.   45
ΚΡ. τί νιν στυγεῖς; πόνων γὰρ ὡς ἁπλῷ λόγῳ
     τῶν νῦν παρόντων οὐδὲν αἰτία τέχνη.
ΗΦ. ἔμπας τὶς αὐτὴν ἄλλος ὤφελεν λαχεῖν.
ΚΡ. ἅπαντ' ἐπαχθῆ πλὴν θεοῖσι κοιρανεῖν·
     ἐλεύθερος γὰρ οὔτις ἐστὶ πλὴν Διός.   50
ΗΦ. ἔγνωκα τοῖσδε κοὐδὲν ἀντειπεῖν ἔχω.
ΚΡ. οὔκουν ἐπείξει δεσμὰ τῷδε περιβαλεῖν,
     ὡς μή σ' ἐλινύοντα προσδερχθῇ πατήρ;

→ ΗΦ. καὶ δὴ πρόχειρα ψάλια δέρκεσθαι πάρα.

ΚΡ. λαβών νιν ἀμφὶ χερσὶν ἐγκρατεῖ σθένει   55
ῥαιστῆρι θεῖνε, πασσάλευε πρὸς πέτραις.

ΗΦ. περαίνεται δὴ κοὐ ματᾷ τοὔργον τόδε.

ΚΡ. ἄρασσε μᾶλλον, σφίγγε, μηδαμῆ χάλα.
δεινὸς γὰρ εὑρεῖν κἀξ ἀμηχάνων πόρον.

↯ ΗΦ. ἄραρεν ἥδε γ᾽ ὠλένη δυσεκλύτως.   60

ΚΡ. καὶ τήνδε νῦν πόρπασον ἀσφαλῶς, ἵνα
μάθῃ σοφιστὴς ὢν Διὸς νωθέστερος.

ΗΦ. πλὴν τοῦδ᾽ ἂν οὐδεὶς ἐνδίκως μέμψαιτό μοι.

ΚΡ. ἀδαμαντίνου νῦν σφηνὸς αὐθάδη γνάθον
στέρνων διαμπὰξ πασσάλευ᾽ ἐρρωμένως.   65

ΗΦ. αἰαῖ, Προμηθεῦ, σῶν ὕπερ στένω πόνων.

ΚΡ. σὺ δ᾽ αὖ κατοκνεῖς τῶν Διός τ᾽ ἐχθρῶν ὕπερ
στένεις; ὅπως μὴ σαυτὸν οἰκτιεῖς ποτέ.

ΗΦ. ὁρᾷς θέαμα δυσθέατον ὄμμασιν.

ΚΡ. ὁρῶ κυροῦντα τόνδε τῶν ἐπαξίων.   70
ἀλλ᾽ ἀμφὶ πλευραῖς μασχαλιστῆρας βάλε.

ΗΦ. δρᾶν ταῦτ᾽ ἀνάγκη, μηδὲν ἐγκέλευ᾽ ἄγαν.

ΚΡ. ἦ μὴν κελεύσω κἀπιθωΰξω γε πρός.
χώρει κάτω, σκέλη δὲ κίρκωσον βίᾳ.

ΗΦ. καὶ δὴ πέπρακται τοὔργον οὐ μακρῷ πόνῳ.   75

ΚΡ. ἐρρωμένως νῦν θεῖνε διατόρους πέδας·
ὡς οὑπιτιμητής γε τῶν ἔργων βαρύς.

ΗΦ. ὅμοια μορφῇ γλῶσσά σου γηρύεται.

ΚΡ. σὺ μαλθακίζου, τὴν δ᾽ ἐμὴν αὐθαδίαν
ὀργῆς τε τραχύτητα μὴ 'πίπλησσέ μοι.   80

ΗΦ. στείχωμεν, ὡς κώλοισιν ἀμφίβληστρ᾽ ἔχει.

ΚΡ. ἐνταῦθα νῦν ὕβριζε, καὶ θεῶν γέρα
συλῶν ἐφημέροισι προστίθει. τί σοι
οἷοί τε θνητοὶ τῶνδ᾽ ἀπαντλῆσαι πόνων;
ψευδωνύμως σε δαίμονες Προμηθέα   85

καλοῦσιν· αὐτὸν γάρ σε δεῖ προμηθέως,
ὅτῳ τρόπῳ τῆσδ' ἐκκυλισθήσει τέχνης.

ΠΡΟΜΗΘΕΥΣ.

ὦ δῖος αἰθὴρ καὶ ταχύπτεροι πνοαὶ,
ποταμῶν τε πηγαὶ, ποντίων τε κυμάτων
ἀνήριθμον γέλασμα, παμμῆτόρ τε γῆ,   90
καὶ τὸν πανόπτην κύκλον ἡλίου καλῶ·
ἴδεσθέ μ' οἷα πρὸς θεῶν πάσχω θεός.
δέρχθηθ' οἵαις αἰκίαισιν
διακναιόμενος τὸν μυριετῆ
χρόνον ἀθλεύσω.   95
τοιόνδ' ὁ νέος ταγὸς μακάρων
ἐξηῦρ' ἐπ' ἐμοὶ δεσμὸν ἀεικῆ.
φεῦ φεῦ, τὸ παρὸν τό τ' ἐπερχόμενον
πῆμα στενάχω, πῇ ποτε μόχθων
χρὴ τέρματα τῶνδ' ἐπιτεῖλαι.   100
καίτοι τί φημί; πάντα προὐξεπίσταμαι
σκεθρῶς τὰ μέλλοντ', οὐδέ μοι ποταίνιον
πῆμ' οὐδὲν ἥξει. τὴν πεπρωμένην δὲ χρὴ
αἶσαν φέρειν ὡς ῥᾷστα, γιγνώσκονθ' ὅτι
τὸ τῆς ἀνάγκης ἔστ' ἀδήριτον σθένος.   105
ἀλλ' οὔτε σιγᾶν οὔτε μὴ σιγᾶν τύχας
οἷόν τέ μοι τάσδ' ἐστί. θνητοῖς γὰρ γέρα
πορὼν ἀνάγκαις ταῖσδ' ἐνέζευγμαι τάλας·
ναρθηκοπλήρωτον δὲ θηρῶμαι πυρὸς
πηγὴν κλοπαίαν, ἣ διδάσκαλος τέχνης   110
πάσης βροτοῖς πέφηνε καὶ μέγας πόρος.
τοιῶνδε ποινὰς ἀμπλακημάτων τίνω,
ὑπαιθρίοις δεσμοῖσι πασσαλευτὸς ὤν.
ἆ ἆ.
τίς ἀχώ, τίς ὀδμὰ προσέπτα μ' ἀφεγγής,   115

θεόσυτος, ἢ βρότειος, ἢ κεκραμένη·
ἵκετο τερμόνιον ἐπὶ πάγον
πόνων ἐμῶν θεωρὸς, ἢ τί δὴ θέλων;
ὁρᾶτε δεσμώτην με δύσποτμον θεὸν,
τὸν Διὸς ἐχθρὸν, τὸν πᾶσι θεοῖς   125
δι' ἀπεχθείας ἐλθόνθ' ὁπόσοι
τὴν Διὸς αὐλὴν εἰσοιχνεῦσιν,
διὰ τὴν λίαν φιλότητα βροτῶν.
φεῦ φεῦ, τί ποτ' αὖ κινάθισμα κλύω
πέλας οἰωνῶν; αἰθὴρ δ' ἐλαφραῖς   130
πτερύγων ῥιπαῖς ὑποσυρίζει.
πᾶν μοι φοβερὸν τὸ προσέρπον.

ΧΟΡΟΣ.

μηδὲν φοβηθῇς· φιλία γὰρ ἥδε τάξις πτερύγων
   θοαῖς ἁμίλλαις προσέβα   στρ. α'
τόνδε πάγον, πατρῴας
μόγις παρειποῦσα φρένας.   135
κραιπνοφόροι δέ μ' ἔπεμψαν αὖραι·
κτύπου γὰρ ἀχὼ χάλυβος διῇξεν ἄντρων μυχὸν.
   ἐκ δ' ἔπληξέ μου
τὰν θεμερῶπιν αἰδῶ·
σύθην δ' ἀπέδιλος ὄχῳ πτερωτῷ.   139

ΠΡ. αἰαῖ αἰαῖ,
τῆς πολυτέκνου Τηθύος ἔκγονα,
τοῦ περὶ πᾶσάν θ' εἱλισσομένου †
χθόν' ἀκοιμήτῳ ῥεύματι παῖδες
πατρὸς Ὠκεανοῦ,   143
δέρχθητ', ἐσίδεσθέ μ' οἵῳ δεσμῷ
προσπορπατὸς
τῆσδε φάραγγος σκοπέλοις ἐν ἄκροις
  ✝ φρουρὰν ἄζηλον ὀχήσω.

ΧΟ. λεύσσω, Προμηθεῦ· φοβερὰ δ' ἐμοῖσιν ὄσσοις
    ὁμίχλα προσῇξε πλήρης δακρύων,   ἀντ. α'
    σὸν δέμας εἰσιδούσᾳ   146
    πέτραις προσαναινόμενον
    ταῖσδ' ἀδαμαντοδέτοισι λύμαις·
    νέοι γὰρ οἰακονόμοι κρατοῦσ' Ὀλύμπου, νεοχμοῖς
    δὲ δὴ νόμοις
    Ζεὺς ἀθέτως κρατύνει.   150
    τὰ πρὶν δὲ πελώρια νῦν ἄϊστοῖ.
ΠΡ. εἰ γάρ μ' ὑπὸ γῆν νέρθεν θ' Ἅιδου
    τοῦ νεκροδέγμονος εἰς ἀπέραντον
    Τάρταρον ἧκεν,
    δεσμοῖς ἀλύτοις ἀγρίοις πελάσας,   155
    ὡς μήτε θεὸς μήτε τις ἄλλος·
    τοῖσδ' ἐπεγήθει.
    νῦν δ' αἰθέριον κίνυγμ' ὁ τάλας
    ἐχθροῖς ἐπίχαρτα πέπονθα.
ΧΟ. τίς ὧδε τλησικάρδιος ·   στρ. β'
    θεῶν ὅτῳ τάδ' ἐπιχαρῇ ;   160
    τίς οὐ ξυνασχαλᾷ κακοῖς
    τεοῖσι, δίχα γε Διός ; ὁ δ' ἐπικότως ἀεὶ
    θέμενος ἄγναμπτον νόον
    δάμναται οὐρανίαν
    γένναν, οὐδὲ λήξει, πρὶν ἂν ἢ κορέσῃ κέαρ, ἢ
    παλάμᾳ τινὶ   165
    τὰν δυσάλωτον ἕλῃ τις ἀρχάν.
ΠΡ. ἦ μὴν ἔτ' ἐμοῦ, καίπερ κρατεραῖς
    ἐν γυιοπέδαις αἰκιζομένου,
    χρείαν ἕξει μακάρων πρύτανις,
    δεῖξαι τὸ νέον βούλευμ' ὑφ' ὅτου   170
    σκῆπτρον τιμάς τ' ἀποσυλᾶται.
    καί μ' οὔτι μελιγλώσσοις πειθοῦς

ἐπαοιδαῖσιν
θέλξει, στερεάς τ' οὔποτ' ἀπειλὰς
πτήξας τόδ' ἐγὼ καταμηνύσω,   175
πρὶν ἂν ἐξ ἀγρίων δεσμῶν χαλάσῃ,
ποινάς τε τίνειν
τῆσδ' αἰκίας ἐθελήσῃ.

ΧΟ. σὺ μὲν θρασύς τε καὶ πικραῖς   ἀντ. β'
δύαισιν οὐδὲν ἐπιχαλᾷς,
ἄγαν δ' ἐλευθεροστομεῖς.   180
ἐμὰς δὲ φρένας ἐρέθισε διατόρος φόβος·
δέδια δ' ἀμφὶ σαῖς τύχαις,
πᾷ ποτε τῶνδε πόνων
χρή σε τέρμα κέλσαντ' ἐσιδεῖν. ἀκίχητα γὰρ ἤθεα
    καὶ κέαρ
ἀπαράμυθον ἔχει Κρόνου παῖς.   185

ΠΡ. οἶδ' ὅτι τραχὺς καὶ παρ' ἑαυτῷ
τὸ δίκαιον ἔχων Ζεύς· ἀλλ' ἔμπας
μαλακογνώμων
ἔσται ποθ', ὅταν ταύτῃ ῥαισθῇ·
τὴν δ' ἀτέραμνον στορέσας ὀργὴν   190
εἰς ἀρθμὸν ἐμοὶ καὶ φιλότητα
σπεύδων σπεύδοντί ποθ' ἥξει.

ΧΟ. πάντ' ἐκκάλυψον καὶ γέγων' ἡμῖν λόγον,
ποίῳ λαβών σε Ζεὺς ἐπ' αἰτιάματι
οὕτως ἀτίμως καὶ πικρῶς αἰκίζεται·   195
δίδαξον ἡμᾶς, εἴ τι μὴ βλάπτει λόγῳ.

ΠΡ. ἀλγεινὰ μέν μοι καὶ λέγειν ἐστὶν τάδε,
ἄλγος δὲ σιγᾶν, πανταχῇ δὲ δύσποτμα.
ἐπεὶ τάχιστ' ἤρξαντο δαίμονες χόλου
στάσις τ' ἐν ἀλλήλοισιν ὠροθύνετο,   200
οἱ μὲν θέλοντες ἐκβαλεῖν ἕδρας Κρόνον,
ὡς Ζεὺς ἀνάσσοι δῆθεν, οἱ δὲ τοὔμπαλιν

σπεύδοντες, ὡς Ζεὺς μήποτ' ἄρξειεν θεῶν,
ἐνταῦθ' ἐγὼ τὰ λῶστα βουλεύων πιθεῖν
Τιτᾶνας, Οὐρανοῦ τε καὶ Χθονὸς τέκνα,   205
οὐκ ἠδυνήθην· αἱμύλας δὲ μηχανὰς
ἀτιμάσαντες καρτεροῖς φρονήμασιν
ᾤοντ' ἀμοχθὶ πρὸς βίαν τε δεσπόσειν·
ἐμοὶ δὲ μήτηρ οὐχ ἅπαξ μόνον Θέμις
καὶ Γαῖα, πολλῶν ὀνομάτων μορφὴ μία,   210
τὸ μέλλον ᾗ κραίνοιτο προὐτεθεσπίκει,
ὡς οὐ κατ' ἰσχὺν οὐδὲ πρὸς τὸ καρτερὸν
χρείη, δόλῳ δὲ τοὺς ὑπερσχόντας κρατεῖν.
τοιαῦτ' ἐμοῦ λόγοισιν ἐξηγουμένου
οὐκ ἠξίωσαν οὐδὲ προσβλέψαι τὸ πᾶν.   215
κράτιστα δή μοι τῶν παρεστώτων τότε
ἐφαίνετ' εἶναι προσλαβόντα μητέρα
ἑκόνθ' ἑκόντι Ζηνὶ συμπαραστατεῖν.
ἐμαῖς δὲ βουλαῖς Ταρτάρου μελαμβαθὴς
κευθμὼν καλύπτει τὸν παλαιγενῆ Κρόνον   220
αὐτοῖσι συμμάχοισι. τοιάδ' ἐξ ἐμοῦ
ὁ τῶν θεῶν τύραννος ὠφελημένος
κακαῖσι ποιναῖς ταῖσδέ μ' ἀντημείψατο.
ἔνεστι γάρ πως τοῦτο τῇ τυραννίδι
νόσημα, τοῖς φίλοισι μὴ πεποιθέναι.   225
ὃ δ' οὖν ἐρωτᾶτ', αἰτίαν καθ' ἥντινα
αἰκίζεταί με, τοῦτο δὴ σαφηνιῶ.
ὅπως τάχιστα τὸν πατρῷον ἐς θρόνον
καθέζετ', εὐθὺς δαίμοσιν νέμει γέρα
ἄλλοισιν ἄλλα καὶ διεστοιχίζετο   230
ἀρχήν· βροτῶν δὲ τῶν ταλαιπώρων λόγον
οὐκ ἔσχεν οὐδέν', ἀλλ' ἀϊστώσας γένος
τὸ πᾶν ἔχρῃζεν ἄλλο φιτῦσαι νέον.
καὶ τοισίδ' οὐδεὶς ἀντέβαινε πλὴν ἐμοῦ.

ἐγὼ δ᾽ ἐτόλμησ᾽· ἐξελυσάμην βροτοὺς   235
τοῦ μὴ <u>διαρραισθέντας</u> εἰς Ἅιδου μολεῖν.
τῷ τοι τοιαῖσδε πημοναῖσι <u>κάμπτομαι</u>,
πάσχειν μὲν ἀλγειναῖσιν, οἰκτραῖσιν δ᾽ ἰδεῖν·
θνητοὺς δ᾽ <u>ἐν οἴκτῳ</u> προθέμενος, τούτου τυχεῖν
οὐκ ἠξιώθην αὐτός, ἀλλὰ νηλεῶς ☩   240
☩ ὧδ᾽ <u>ἐρρύθμισμαι</u>, Ζηνὶ <u>δυσκλεὴς</u> θέα.

ΧΟ. σιδηρόφρων τε κἀκ πέτρας εἰργασμένος
    ὅστις, Προμηθεῦ, σοῖσιν οὐ ξυνασχαλᾷ
    μόχθοις· ἐγὼ γὰρ οὔτ᾽ ἂν εἰσιδεῖν τάδε
    ἔχρῃζον εἰσιδοῦσά τ᾽ ἠλγύνθην κέαρ.   245
ΠΡ. καὶ μὴν φίλοις <u>ἐλεινὸς</u> εἰσορᾶν ἐγώ.
ΧΟ. μή πού τι <u>προὔβης</u> τῶνδε καὶ περαιτέρω ;
ΠΡ. θνητοὺς ἔπαυσα μὴ <u>προδέρκεσθαι</u> μόρον.
ΧΟ. τὸ ποῖον εὑρὼν τῆσδε φάρμακον νόσου ;
ΠΡ. τυφλὰς ἐν αὐτοῖς ἐλπίδας κατῴκισα.   250
ΧΟ. μέγ᾽ ὠφέλημα τοῦτ᾽ ἐδωρήσω βροτοῖς.
ΠΡ. πρὸς τοῖσδε μέντοι πῦρ ἐγώ σφιν ὤπασα.
ΧΟ. καὶ νῦν φλογωπὸν πῦρ ἔχουσ᾽ ἐφήμεροι ;
ΠΡ. ἀφ᾽ οὗ γε πολλὰς ἐκμαθήσονται τέχνας.
ΧΟ. τοιοῖσδε δή σε Ζεὺς ἐπ᾽ αἰτιάμασιν   255
    αἰκίζεταί τε κοὐδαμῇ χαλᾷ κακῶν,
    οὐδ᾽ ἔστιν ἄθλου τέρμα σοι <u>προκείμενον</u> ;
ΠΡ. οὐκ ἄλλο γ᾽ οὐδέν, πλὴν ὅταν κείνῳ δοκῇ.
ΧΟ. δόξει δὲ πῶς ; τίς ἐλπίς ; οὐχ ὁρᾷς ὅτι
    ἥμαρτες ; ὡς δ᾽ ἥμαρτες οὔτ᾽ ἐμοὶ λέγειν   260
    <u>καθ᾽ ἡδονὴν</u> σοί τ᾽ ἄλγος. ἀλλὰ ταῦτα μὲν
    μεθῶμεν, ἄθλων δ᾽ ἔκλυσιν ζήτει τινά.
ΠΡ. ἐλαφρὸν ὅστις πημάτων ἔξω πόδα
    ἔχει <u>παραινεῖν νουθετεῖν</u> τε τὸν κακῶς
    πράσσοντ᾽· ἐγὼ δὲ ταῦθ᾽ ἅπαντ᾽ ἠπιστάμην.   265
    ἑκὼν ἑκὼν ἥμαρτον, οὐκ ἀρνήσομαι·

θνητοῖς δ' ἀρήγων αὐτὸς ηὑρόμην πόνους.
οὐ μήν τι ποιναῖς γ' ᾠόμην τοίαισί με
κατισχνανεῖσθαι πρὸς πέτραις πεδαρσίοις,
τυχόντ' ἐρήμου τοῦδ' ἀγείτονος πάγου.   270
καί μοι τὰ μὲν παρόντα μὴ δύρεσθ' ἄχη,
πέδοι δὲ βᾶσαι τὰς προσερπούσας τύχας
ἀκούσαθ', ὡς μάθητε διὰ τέλους τὸ πᾶν.
πίθεσθέ μοι, πίθεσθε, συμπονήσατε
τῷ νῦν μογοῦντι. ταῦτά τοι πλανωμένη   275
πρὸς ἄλλοτ' ἄλλον πημονὴ προσιζάνει.

ΧΟ. οὐκ ἀκούσαις ἐπεθώϋξας
τοῦτο, Προμηθεῦ.
καὶ νῦν ἐλαφρῷ ποδὶ κραιπνόσυτον
θᾶκον προλιποῦσ',   280
αἰθέρα θ' ἁγνὸν πόρον οἰωνῶν,
ὀκριοέσσῃ χθονὶ τῇδε πελῶ·
τοὺς σοὺς δὲ πόνους
χρῄζω διὰ παντὸς ἀκοῦσαι.

ΩΚΕΑΝΟΣ.

ἥκω δολιχῆς τέρμα κελεύθου
διαμειψάμενος πρὸς σὲ, Προμηθεῦ,   285
τὸν πτερυγωκῆ τόνδ' οἰωνὸν
γνώμῃ στομίων ἄτερ εὐθύνων·
ταῖς σαῖς δὲ τύχαις, ἴσθι, συναλγῶ.
τό τε γάρ με, δοκῶ, ξυγγενὲς οὕτως
ἐσαναγκάζει,   290
χωρίς τε γένους οὐκ ἔστιν ὅτῳ
μείζονα μοῖραν νείμαιμ' ἢ σοί.
γνώσει δὲ τάδ' ὡς ἔτυμ', οὐδὲ μάτην
χαριτογλωσσεῖν ἔνι μοι· φέρε γὰρ

σήμαιν' ὅ τι χρή σοι ξυμπράσσειν·   295
οὐ γάρ ποτ' ἐρεῖς ὡς Ὠκεανοῦ
φίλος ἐστὶ βεβαιότερός σοι.

ΠΡ. ἔα, τί χρῆμά; καὶ σὺ δὴ πόνων ἐμῶν
ἥκεις ἐπόπτης; πῶς ἐτόλμησας, λιπὼν
ἐπώνυμόν τε ῥεῦμα καὶ πετρηρεφῆ   300
αὐτόκτιτ' ἄντρα, τὴν σιδηρομήτορα
ἐλθεῖν ἐς αἶαν; ἢ θεωρήσων τύχας
ἐμὰς ἀφῖξαι καὶ ξυνασχαλῶν κακοῖς;
δέρκου θέαμα, τόνδε τὸν Διὸς φίλον,
τὸν ξυγκαταστήσαντα τὴν τυραννίδα,   305
οἵαις ὑπ' αὐτοῦ πημοναῖσι κάμπτομαι.

ΩΚ. ὁρῶ, Προμηθεῦ, καὶ παραινέσαι γέ τοι
θέλω τὰ λῷστα, καίπερ ὄντι ποικίλῳ.
γίγνωσκε σαυτὸν καὶ μεθάρμοσαι τρόπους
νέους· νέος γὰρ καὶ τύραννος ἐν θεοῖς.   310
εἰ δ' ὧδε τραχεῖς καὶ τεθηγμένους λόγους
ῥίψεις, τάχ' ἄν σου καὶ μακρὰν ἀνωτέρω
θακῶν κλύοι Ζεύς, ὥστε σοι τὸν νῦν ὄχλον
παρόντα μόχθων παιδιὰν εἶναι δοκεῖν.
ἀλλ', ὦ ταλαίπωρ', ἃς ἔχεις ὀργὰς ἄφες,   315
ζήτει δὲ τῶνδε πημάτων ἀπαλλαγάς.
ἀρχαῖ' ἴσως σοι φαίνομαι λέγειν τάδε·
τοιαῦτα μέντοι τῆς ἄγαν ὑψηγόρου
γλώσσης, Προμηθεῦ, τἀπίχειρα γίγνεται.
σὺ δ' οὐδέπω ταπεινὸς οὐδ' εἴκεις κακοῖς,   320
πρὸς τοῖς παροῦσι δ' ἄλλα προσλαβεῖν θέλεις.
οὔκουν ἔμοιγε χρώμενος διδασκάλῳ
πρὸς κέντρα κῶλον ἐκτενεῖς, ὁρῶν ὅτι
τραχὺς μόναρχος οὐδ' ὑπεύθυνος κρατεῖ.
καὶ νῦν ἐγὼ μὲν εἶμι καὶ πειράσομαι   325
ἐὰν δύνωμαι τῶνδέ σ' ἐκλῦσαι πόνων·

σὺ δ' ἡσύχαζε μηδ' ἄγαν λαβροστόμει.
ἢ οὐκ οἶσθ' ἀκριβῶς ὢν περισσόφρων ὅτι
γλώσσῃ ματαίᾳ ζημία προστρίβεται ;
ΠΡ. ζηλῶ σ' ὁθούνεκ' ἐκτὸς αἰτίας κυρεῖς,   330
πάντων μετασχὼν καὶ τετολμηκὼς ἐμοί.
καὶ νῦν ἔασον μηδέ σοι μελησάτω.
πάντως γὰρ οὐ πείσεις νιν· οὐ γὰρ εὐπιθής.
+ πάπταινε δ' αὐτὸς μή τι πημανθῇς ὁδῷ.
ΩΚ. πολλῷ γ' ἀμείνων τοὺς πέλας φρενοῦν ἔφυς   335
ἢ σαυτόν· ἔργῳ κοὐ λόγῳ τεκμαίρομαι.+
ὁρμώμενον δὲ μηδαμῶς μ' ἀντισπάσῃς· +
αὐχῶ γὰρ αὐχῶ τήνδε δωρεὰν ἐμοὶ
δώσειν Δί', ὥστε τῶνδέ σ' ἐκλῦσαι πόνων.
ΠΡ. τὰ μέν σ' ἐπαινῶ κοὐδαμῇ λήξω ποτέ·   340
+ προθυμίας γὰρ οὐδὲν ἐλλείπεις. ἀτὰρ
μηδὲν πόνει· μάτην γὰρ οὐδὲν ὠφελῶν
ἐμοὶ πονήσεις, εἴ τι καὶ πονεῖν θέλεις.
ἀλλ' ἡσύχαζε σαυτὸν ἐκποδὼν ἔχων·
ἐγὼ γὰρ οὐκ εἰ δυστυχῶ, τοῦδ' οὕνεκα   345
θέλοιμ' ἂν ὡς πλείστοισι πημονὰς τυχεῖν.
οὐ δῆτ', ἐπεί με χαὶ κασιγνήτου τύχαι
τείρουσ' Ἄτλαντος, ὃς πρὸς ἑσπέρους τόπους
ἕστηκε κίον' οὐρανοῦ τε καὶ χθονὸς
ὤμοις ἐρείδων, ἄχθος οὐκ εὐάγκαλον.   350
τὸν γηγενῆ τε Κιλικίων οἰκήτορα
ἄντρων ἰδὼν ᾤκτειρα, δάϊον τέρας,
ἑκατογκάρανον πρὸς βίαν χειρούμενον
Τυφῶνα θοῦρον, πᾶσιν ὃς ἀνέστη θεοῖς,
σμερδναῖσι γαμφηλαῖσι συρίζων φόνον·   355
ἐξ ὀμμάτων δ' ἤστραπτε γοργωπὸν σέλας,
ὡς τὴν Διὸς τυραννίδ' ἐκπέρσων βίᾳ·
ἀλλ' ἦλθεν αὐτῷ Ζηνὸς ἄγρυπνον βέλος,

✝ καταιβάτης κεραυνὸς ἐκπνέων φλόγα,
ὃς αὐτὸν ἐξέπληξε τῶν ὑψηγόρων   360
κομπασμάτων. φρένας γὰρ εἰς αὐτὰς τυπεὶς
ἐφεψαλώθη κἀξεβροντήθη σθένος.
καὶ νῦν ἀχρεῖον καὶ παράορον δέμας
κεῖται στενωπαῦ πλησίον θαλασσίου
ἱπούμενος ῥίζαισιν Αἰτναίαις ὕπο·   365
κορυφαῖς δ᾽ ἐν ἄκραις ἥμενος μυδροκτυπεῖ
Ἥφαιστος, ἔνθεν ἐκραγήσονταί ποτε
ποταμοὶ πυρὸς δάπτοντες ἀγρίαις γνάθοις
τῆς καλλικάρπου Σικελίας λευροὺς γύας·
τοιόνδε Τυφὼς ἐξαναζέσει χόλον   370
θερμῆς ἀπλήστου βέλεσι πυρπνόου ζάλης,
καίπερ κεραυνῷ Ζηνὸς ἠνθρακωμένος.
σὺ δ᾽ οὐκ ἄπειρος, οὐδ᾽ ἐμοῦ διδασκάλου
χρήζεις· σεαυτὸν σῶζ᾽ ὅπως ἐπίστασαι·
ἐγὼ δὲ τὴν παροῦσαν ἀντλήσω τύχην,   375
ἔς τ᾽ ἂν Διὸς φρόνημα λωφήσῃ χόλου.

ΩΚ. οὔκουν, Προμηθεῦ, τοῦτο γιγνώσκεις ὅτι
ὀργῆς ζεούσης εἰσὶν ἰατροὶ λόγοι ;

ΠΡ. ἐάν τις ἐν καιρῷ γε μαλθάσσῃ κέαρ
καὶ μὴ σφριγῶντα θυμὸν ἰσχναίνῃ βίᾳ.   380

ΩΚ. ἐν τῷ προμηθεῖσθαι δὲ καὶ τολμᾶν τίνα ✝
ὁρᾷς ἐνοῦσαν ζημίαν; δίδασκέ με.

ΠΡ. μόχθον περισσὸν κουφόνουν τ᾽ εὐηθίαν. ✝

ΩΚ. ἔα με τήνδε τὴν νόσον νοσεῖν, ἐπεὶ
κέρδιστον εὖ φρονοῦντα μὴ δοκεῖν φρονεῖν.   385

ΠΡ. ἐμὸν δοκήσει τἀμπλάκημ᾽ εἶναι τόδε.

ΩΚ. σαφῶς μ᾽ ἐς οἶκον σὸς λόγος στέλλει πάλιν.

ΠΡ. μὴ γάρ σε θρῆνος οὑμὸς εἰς ἔχθραν βάλῃ.

ΩΚ. ἦ τῷ νέον θακοῦντι παγκρατεῖς ἕδρας ;

ΠΡ. τούτου φυλάσσου μή ποτ᾽ ἀχθεσθῇ κέαρ.   390

✝

ΩΚ. ἡ σὴ, Προμηθεῦ, ξυμφορὰ διδάσκαλος.

ΠΡ. στέλλου, κομίζου, σῶζε τὸν παρόντα νοῦν.

ΩΚ. ὁρμωμένῳ μοι τόνδ' ἐθώϋξας λόγον.
    λευρὸν γὰρ οἶμον αἰθέρος ψαίρει πτεροῖς
    τετρασκελὴς οἰωνός· ἄσμενος δέ τἂν   395
    σταθμοῖς ἐν οἰκείοισι κάμψειεν γόνυ.

ΧΟ. στένω σε τᾶς οὐλομένας τύχας, Προμηθεῦ,   στρ. α'
    δακρυσίστακτον δ' ἀπ' ὄσσων ῥαδινῶν λειβομένα
    ῥέος παρειὰν   400
    νοτίοις ἔτεγξα παγαῖς· ἀμέγαρτα γὰρ τάδε Ζεὺς
    ἰδίοις νόμοις κρατύνων ὑπερήφανον θεοῖς τοῖς
    πάρος ἐνδείκνυσιν αἰχμάν.   405
    πρόπασα δ' ἤδη στονόεν λέλακε χώρα,   ἀντ. α'
    μεγαλοσχήμονά τ' ἀρχαιοπρεπῆ * ∪ ∪ * στένουσι
    τὰν σὰν
    ξυνομαιμόνων τε τιμὰν, ὁπόσοι τ' ἔποικον ἁγνᾶς
    Ἀσίας ἕδος νέμονται, μεγαλοστόνοισι σοῖς πήμασι
    συγκάμνουσι θνατοί·
    Κολχίδος τε γᾶς ἔνοικοι   στρ. β' 415
    παρθένοι, μάχας ἄτρεστοι,
    καὶ Σκύθης ὅμιλος, οἳ γᾶς
    ἔσχατον τόπον ἀμφὶ Μαιῶτιν ἔχουσι λίμναν,
    Ἀραβίας τ' Ἄρειον ἄνθος,   ἀντ. β' 420
    ὑψίκρημνόν θ' οἳ πόλισμα
    Καυκάσου πέλας νέμονται,
    δάϊος στρατὸς, ὀξυπρῴροισι βρέμων ἐν αἰχμαῖς.
    μόνον δὴ πρόσθεν ἄλλον ἐν πόνοις   425
    δαμέντ' ἀδαμαντοδέτοις Τιτᾶνα λύμαις
    εἰσιδόμαν θεὸν Ἄτλανθ',
    ὃς αἰὲν ὑπέροχον σθένος κραταιὸν
    γᾶς οὐράνιόν τε πόλον νώτοις ὑποστενάζει.   430
    βοᾷ δὲ πόντιος κλύδων

ξυμπίτνων, στένει βυθὸς,
κελαινὸς Ἄϊδος δ᾽ ὑποβρέμει μυχὸς γᾶς,
παγαί θ᾽ ἁγνορύτων ποταμῶν στένουσιν ἄλγος
οἰκτρόν. 435

ΠΡ. μή τοι χλιδῇ δοκεῖτε μηδ᾽ αὐθαδίᾳ
σιγᾶν με· συννοίᾳ δὲ δάπτομαι κέαρ,
ὁρῶν ἐμαυτὸν ὧδε προυσελούμενον.
καίτοι θεοῖσι τοῖς νέοις τούτοις γέρα
τίς ἄλλος ἢ 'γὼ παντελῶς διώρισεν; 440
ἀλλ᾽ αὐτὰ σιγῶ. καὶ γὰρ εἰδυίαισιν ἂν
ὑμῖν λέγοιμι· τἀν βροτοῖς δὲ πήματα
ἀκούσαθ᾽, ὡς σφᾶς νηπίους ὄντας τὸ πρὶν
ἔννους ἔθηκα καὶ φρενῶν ἐπηβόλους.
λέξω δὲ, μέμψιν οὔτιν᾽ ἀνθρώποις ἔχων, 445
ἀλλ᾽ ὧν δέδωκ᾽ εὔνοιαν ἐξηγούμενος·
οἳ πρῶτα μὲν βλέποντες ἔβλεπον μάτην,
κλύοντες οὐκ ἤκουον, ἀλλ᾽ ὀνειράτων
ἀλίγκιοι μορφαῖσι τὸν μακρὸν χρόνον
ἔφυρον εἰκῇ πάντα, κοὔτε πλινθυφεῖς 450
δόμους προσείλους ᾖσαν, οὐ ξυλουργίαν·
κατώρυχες δ᾽ ἔναιον ὥστ᾽ ἀήσυροι
μύρμηκες ἄντρων ἐν μυχοῖς ἀνηλίοις.
ἦν δ᾽ οὐδὲν αὐτοῖς οὔτε χείματος τέκμαρ
οὔτ᾽ ἀνθεμώδους ἦρος οὔτε καρπίμου 455
θέρους βέβαιον, ἀλλ᾽ ἄτερ γνώμης τὸ πᾶν
ἔπρασσον, ἔς τε δή σφιν ἀντολὰς ἐγὼ
ἄστρων ἔδειξα τάς τε δυσκρίτους δύσεις.
καὶ μὴν ἀριθμὸν ἔξοχον σοφισμάτων
ἐξηῦρον αὐτοῖς, γραμμάτων τε συνθέσεις, 460
μνήμην θ᾽ ἁπάντων μουσομήτορ᾽ ἐργάτιν.
κἄζευξα πρῶτος ἐν ζυγοῖσι κνώδαλα
ζεύγλαισι δουλεύοντα· σώμασίν θ᾽ ὅπως

c

θνητοῖς μεγίστων διάδοχοι μοχθημάτων
γένοινθ', ὑφ' ἅρματ' ἤγαγον φιληνίους   465
ἵππους, ἄγαλμα τῆς ὑπερπλούτου χλιδῆς.
θαλασσόπλαγκτα δ' οὔτις ἄλλος ἀντ' ἐμοῦ
λινόπτερ' ηὗρε ναυτίλων ὀχήματα.
τοιαῦτα μηχανήματ' ἐξευρὼν τάλας
βροτοῖσιν, αὐτὸς οὐκ ἔχω σόφισμ' ὅτῳ   470
τῆς νῦν παρούσης πημονῆς ἀπαλλαγῶ.

ΧΟ. πέπονθας αἰκὲς πῆμ'· ἀποσφαλεὶς φρενῶν
πλανᾷ, κακὸς δ' ἰατρὸς ὥς τις ἐς νόσον
πεσὼν ἀθυμεῖς καὶ σεαυτὸν οὐκ ἔχεις
εὑρεῖν ὁποίοις φαρμάκοις ἰάσιμος.·   475

ΠΡ. τὰ λοιπά μου κλύουσα θαυμάσει πλέον,
οἵας τέχνας τε καὶ πόρους ἐμησάμην.
τὸ μὲν μέγιστον, εἴ τις ἐς νόσον πέσοι,
οὐκ ἦν ἀλέξημ' οὐδὲν οὔτε βρώσιμον,
οὐ χριστόν, οὔτε πιστόν, ἀλλὰ φαρμάκων   480
χρείᾳ κατεσκέλλοντο, πρίν γ' ἐγὼ σφίσιν
ἔδειξα κράσεις ἠπίων ἀκεσμάτων,
αἷς τὰς ἀπάσας ἐξαμύνονται νόσους.
τρόπους τε πολλοὺς μαντικῆς ἐστοίχισα,
κἄκρινα πρῶτος ἐξ ὀνειράτων ἃ χρὴ   485
ὕπαρ γενέσθαι, κληδόνας τε δυσκρίτους
ἐγνώρισ' αὐτοῖς· ἐνοδίους τε συμβόλους
γαμψωνύχων τε πτῆσιν οἰωνῶν σκεθρῶς
διώρισ', οἵτινές τε δεξιοὶ φύσιν
εὐωνύμους τε, καὶ δίαιταν ἥντινα   490
ἔχουσ' ἕκαστοι, καὶ πρὸς ἀλλήλους τίνες
ἔχθραι τε καὶ στέργηθρα καὶ ξυνεδρίαι·
σπλάγχνων τε λειότητα, καὶ χροιὰν τίνα
ἔχοντ' ἂν εἴη δαίμοσιν πρὸς ἡδονὴν,
χολῆς λοβοῦ τε ποικίλην εὐμορφίαν,   495

κνίσῃ τε κῶλα ξυγκαλυπτὰ καὶ μακρὰν
ὀσφῦν πυρώσας δυστέκμαρτον ἐς τέχνην
ὥδωσα θνητούς· καὶ φλογωπὰ σήματα
ἐξωμμάτωσα, πρόσθεν ὄντ᾽ ἐπάργεμα.
τοιαῦτα μὲν δὴ ταῦτ᾽· ἔνερθε δὲ χθονὸς   500
κεκρυμμέν᾽ ἀνθρώποισιν ὠφελήματα,
χαλκὸν, σίδηρον, ἄργυρον, χρυσόν τε τίς
φήσειεν ἂν πάροιθεν ἐξευρεῖν ἐμοῦ ;
οὐδεὶς, σάφ᾽ οἶδα, μὴ μάτην φλῦσαι θέλων.
βραχεῖ δὲ μύθῳ πάντα συλλήβδην μάθε,   505
πᾶσαι τέχναι βροτοῖσιν ἐκ Προμηθέως.

ΧΟ. μή νυν βροτοὺς μὲν ὠφέλει καιροῦ πέρα,
σαυτοῦ δ᾽ ἀκήδει δυστυχοῦντος· ὡς ἐγὼ
εὔελπίς εἰμι τῶνδέ σ᾽ ἐκ δεσμῶν ἔτι
λυθέντα μηδὲν μεῖον ἰσχύσειν Διός.   510

ΠΡ. οὐ ταῦτα ταύτῃ Μοῖρά πω τελεσφόρος
κρᾶναι πέπρωται, μυρίαις δὲ πημοναῖς
δύαις τε καμφθεὶς ὧδε δεσμὰ φυγγάνω·
τέχνη δ᾽ ἀνάγκης ἀσθενεστέρα μακρῷ.

ΧΟ. τίς οὖν ἀνάγκης ἐστὶν οἰακοστρόφος ;   515

ΠΡ. Μοῖραι τρίμορφοι μνήμονές τ᾽ Ἐρινύες.

ΧΟ. τούτων ἄρα Ζεύς ἐστιν ἀσθενέστερος.

ΠΡ. οὔκουν ἂν ἐκφύγοι γε τὴν πεπρωμένην.

ΧΟ. τί γὰρ πέπρωται Ζηνὶ πλὴν ἀεὶ κρατεῖν ;

ΠΡ. τοῦτ᾽ οὐκέτ᾽ ἂν πύθοιο μηδὲ λιπάρει.   520

ΧΟ. ἦ πού τι σεμνόν ἐστιν ὃ ξυναμπέχεις.

ΠΡ. ἄλλου λόγου μέμνησθε, τόνδε δ᾽ οὐδαμῶς
καιρὸς γεγωνεῖν, ἀλλὰ συγκαλυπτέος
ὅσον μάλιστα· τόνδε γὰρ σώζων ἐγὼ
δεσμοὺς ἀεικεῖς καὶ δύας ἐκφυγγάνω.   525

ΧΟ. μηδάμ᾽ ὁ πάντα νέμων   στρ. α´
θεῖτ᾽ ἐμᾷ γνώμᾳ κράτος ἀντίπαλον Ζεὺς,

μηδ' ἐλινύσαιμι θεοὺς ὁσίαις θοίναις ποτινισσομένα 530
βουφόνοις, παρ' Ὠκεανοῦ πατρὸς ἄσβεστον πόρον,
μηδ' ἀλίτοιμι λόγοις,
ἀλλά μοι τόδ' ἐμμένοι καὶ μήποτ' ἐκτακείη ✝ 535
ἡδύ τι θαρσαλέαις   ἀντ. α΄
τὸν μακρὸν τείνειν βίον ἐλπίσι, φαναῖς
θυμὸν ἀλδαίνουσαν ἐν εὐφροσύναις. φρίσσω δέ
σε δερκομένα 540
μυρίοις μόχθοις διακναιόμενον * * *
Ζῆνα γὰρ οὐ τρομέων
αὐτόνῳ γνώμᾳ σέβει θνατοὺς ἄγαν, Προμηθεῦ.
φέρ' ὅπως ἄχαρις χάρις, ὦ φίλος, εἰπὲ, ποῦ τίς
ἀλκά;   στρ. β΄ 545
τίς ἐφαμερίων ἄρηξις; οὐδ' ἐδέρχθης
✝ ὀλιγοδρανίαν ἄκικυν,✝
ἰσόνειρον, ᾇ τὸ φωτῶν
ἀλαὸν γένος ἐμπεποδισμένον; οὔποτε θνατῶν 550
τὰν Διὸς ἁρμονίαν ἀνδρῶν παρεξίασι βουλαί.
ἔμαθον τάδε σὰς προσιδοῦσ' ὀλοὰς τύχας, Προμηθεῦ.   ἀντ. β΄ 553
τὸ διαμφίδιον δέ μοι μέλος προσέπτα 555
τόδ' ἐκεῖνό θ', ὅτ' ἀμφὶ λουτρὰ
καὶ λέχος σὸν ὑμεναίουν
ἰότατι γάμων, ὅτε τὰν ὁμοπάτριον ἕδνοις
ἄγαγες Ἡσιόναν πιθὼν δάμαρτα κοινόλεκτρον. 560

ΙΩ.

τίς γῆ; τί γένος; τίνα φῶ λεύσσειν
τόνδε χαλινοῖς ἐν πετρίνοισιν
χειμαζόμενον;

τίνος ἀμπλακίας ποιναῖς ὀλέκει;
σήμηνον ὅπᾱ ι
γῆς ἢ μογερὰ πεπλάνημαι.   565
ἆ ἆ,
χρίει τις αὖ με τὰν τάλαιναν οἶστρος,
εἴδωλον Ἄργου γηγενοῦς, ἄλευε δᾶ,
τὸν μυριωπὸν εἰσορῶσα βούταν.
ὁ δὲ πορεύεται δόλιον ὄμμ᾽ ἔχων,   570
ὃν οὐδὲ κατθανόντα γαῖα κεύθει.
ἀλλ᾽ ἐμὲ τὰν τάλαιναν
ἐξ ἐνέρων περῶν κυναγετεῖ,
πλανᾷ τε νῆστιν ἀνὰ τὰν παραλίαν ψάμμον.
ὑπὸ δὲ κηρόπλαστος ὀτοβεῖ δόναξ   στρ.
ἀχέτας ὑπνοδόταν νόμον· ἰὼ ἰὼ, πόποι,   575
ποῖ, πόποι, ποῖ μ᾽ ἄγουσι τηλέπλανοι πλάναι;
τί ποτέ μ᾽, ὦ Κρόνιε
παῖ, τί ποτε ταῖσδ᾽ ἐνέζευξας εὑρὼν ἁμαρτοῦσαν
ἐν πημοσύναις, ἐῆ,
οἰστρηλάτῳ δὲ δείματι δειλαίαν   580
παράκοπον ὧδε τείρεις;
πυρί με φλέξον, ἢ χθονὶ κάλυψον, ἢ ποντίοις δάκεσι
δὸς βοράν,
μηδέ μοι φθονήσῃς
εὐγμάτων, ἄναξ.
ἅδην με πολύπλανοι πλάναι   585
γεγυμνάκασιν, οὐδ᾽ ἔχω μαθεῖν ὅπα
πημονὰς ἀλύξω.
κλύεις φθέγμα τᾶς βούκερω παρθένου;
ΠΡ. πῶς δ᾽ οὐ κλύω τῆς οἰστροδινήτου κόρης
τῆς Ἰναχείας; ἢ Διὸς θάλπει κέαρ   590
ἔρωτι, καὶ νῦν τοὺς ὑπερμήκεις δρόμους
Ἥρᾳ στυγητὸς πρὸς βίαν γυμνάζεται.

ΙΩ.　πόθεν ἐμοῦ σὺ πατρὸς ὄνομ' ἀπύεις,　　　　ἀντ.

εἰπέ μοι τᾷ μογερᾷ τίς ὢν τίς ἄρα μ', ὦ τάλας,

τὰν ταλαίπωρον ὧδ' ἐτήτυμα προσθροεῖς,　595

θεόσυτόν τε νόσον

ὠνόμασας, ἃ μαραίνει με χρίουσα κέντροις　＊ ＊

φοιταλέοις, ἐή.

σκιρτημάτων δὲ νήστισιν αἰκίαις　　　　　600

λαβρόσυτος ἦλθον, Ἥρας

ἐπικότοισι μήδεσι δαμεῖσα. δυσδαιμόνων δὲ τίνες

οἳ, ἐή,

οἳ' ἐγὼ μογοῦσιν;

ἀλλά μοι τορῶς

τέκμηρον ὅ τι μ' ἐπαμμένει　　　　　　　605

παθεῖν, τί μῆχαρ, ἢ τί φάρμακον νόσου,

δεῖξον, εἴπερ οἶσθα·

θρόει, φράζε τᾷ δυσπλάνῳ παρθένῳ.

ΠΡ.　λέξω τορῶς σοι πᾶν ὅπερ χρῄζεις μαθεῖν,

οὐκ ἐμπλέκων αἰνίγματ', ἀλλ' ἁπλῷ λόγῳ,　610

ὥσπερ δίκαιον πρὸς φίλους οἴγειν στόμα.

πυρὸς βροτοῖς δοτῆρ' ὁρᾷς Προμηθέα.

ΙΩ.　ὦ κοινὸν ὠφέλημα θνητοῖσιν φανείς,

τλῆμον Προμηθεῦ, τοῦ δίκην πάσχεις τάδε;

ΠΡ.　ἁρμοῖ πέπαυμαι τοὺς ἐμοὺς θρηνῶν πόνους.　615

ΙΩ.　οὔκουν πόροις ἂν τήνδε δωρεὰν ἐμοί;

ΠΡ.　λέγ' ἥντιν' αἰτεῖ· πᾶν γὰρ ἂν πύθοιό μου.

ΙΩ.　σήμηνον ὅστις ἐν φάραγγί σ' ὤχμασε.

ΠΡ.　βούλευμα μὲν τὸ Δῖον, Ἡφαίστου δὲ χείρ.

ΙΩ.　ποινὰς δὲ ποίων ἀμπλακημάτων τίνεις;　620

ΠΡ.　τοσοῦτον ἀρκῶ σοι σαφηνίσαι μόνον.

ΙΩ.　καὶ πρός γε τούτοις τέρμα τῆς ἐμῆς πλάνης

δεῖξον τίς ἔσται τῇ ταλαιπώρῳ χρόνος.

ΠΡ.　τὸ μὴ μαθεῖν σοι κρεῖσσον ἢ μαθεῖν τάδε.

ΙΩ. μήτοι με κρύψῃς τοῦθ' ὅπερ μέλλω παθεῖν. 625
ΠΡ. ἀλλ' οὐ μεγαίρω τοῦδέ σοι δωρήματος. ┴
ΙΩ. τί δῆτα μέλλεις μὴ οὐ γεγωνίσκειν τὸ πᾶν ;
ΠΡ. φθόνος μὲν οὐδείς, σὰς δ' ὀκνῶ θρᾶξαι φρένας.
ΙΩ. μή μου προκήδου μᾶσσον ὡς ἐμοὶ γλυκύ.
ΓΡ. ἐπεὶ προθυμεῖ, χρὴ λέγειν· ἄκουε δή. 630
ΧΟ. μήπω γε· μοῖραν δ' ἡδονῆς κἀμοὶ πόρε.
   τὴν τῆσδε πρῶτον ἱστορήσωμεν νόσον,
   αὐτῆς λεγούσης τὰς πολυφθόρους τύχας·
   τὰ λοιπὰ δ' ἄθλων σοῦ διδαχθήτω πάρα.
ΠΡ. σὸν ἔργον, Ἰοῖ, ταῖσδ' ὑπουργῆσαι χάριν, 635
   ἄλλως τε πάντως καὶ κασιγνήταις πατρός.
   ὡς τἀποκλαῦσαι κἀποδύρασθαι τύχας
   ἐνταῦθ', ὅπῃ μέλλοι τις οἴσεσθαι δάκρυ
   πρὸς τῶν κλυόντων, ἀξίαν τριβὴν ἔχει.
ΙΩ. οὐκ οἶδ' ὅπως ὑμῖν ἀπιστῆσαί με χρή, 640
   σαφεῖ δὲ μύθῳ πᾶν ὅπερ προσχρῄζετε
   πεύσεσθε· καίτοι καὶ λέγουσ' αἰσχύνομαι
   θεόσσυτον χειμῶνα καὶ διαφθορὰν
   μορφῆς, ὅθεν μοι σχετλία προσέπτατο.
   ἀεὶ γὰρ ὄψεις ἔννυχοι πολούμεναι 645
   ἐς παρθενῶνας τοὺς ἐμοὺς παρηγόρουν
   λείοισι μύθοις· ὦ μέγ' εὔδαιμον κόρη,
   τί παρθενεύει δαρόν, ἐξόν σοι γάμου
   τυχεῖν μεγίστου ; Ζεὺς γὰρ ἱμέρου βέλει
   πρὸς σοῦ τέθαλπται καὶ ξυναίρεσθαι Κύπριν 650
   θέλει· σὺ δ', ὦ παῖ, μἀπολακτίσῃς λέχος
   τὸ Ζηνός, ἀλλ' ἔξελθε πρὸς Λέρνης βαθὺν
   λειμῶνα, ποίμνας βουστάσεις τε πρὸς πατρός,
   ὡς ἂν τὸ Δῖον ὄμμα λωφήσῃ πόθου.
   τοιοῖσδε πάσας εὐφρόνας ὀνείρασι 655
   ξυνειχόμην δύστηνος, ἔς τε δὴ πατρὶ

ἔτλην γεγωνεῖν νυκτίφαντ' ὀνείρατα.
ὁ δ' ἔς τε Πυθὼ κἀπὶ Δωδώνης πυκνοὺς
θεοπρόπους ἴαλλεν, ὡς μάθοι τί χρὴ
δρῶντ' ἢ λέγοντα δαίμοσιν πράσσειν φίλα.   660
ἧκον δ' ἀναγγέλλοντες αἰολοστόμους
χρησμοὺς ἀσήμους δυσκρίτως τ' εἰρημένους.
τέλος δ' ἐναργὴς βάξις ἦλθεν Ἰνάχῳ
σαφῶς ἐπισκήπτουσα καὶ μυθουμένη
ἔξω δόμων τε καὶ πάτρας ὠθεῖν ἐμέ,   665
ἄφετον ἀλᾶσθαι γῆς ἐπ' ἐσχάτοις ὅροις·
κεἰ μὴ θέλοι, πυρωπὸν ἐκ Διὸς μολεῖν
κεραυνόν, ὃς πᾶν ἐξαϊστώσοι γένος.
τοιοῖσδε πεισθεὶς Λοξίου μαντεύμασιν,
ἐξήλασέν με κἀπέκλῃσε δωμάτων   670
ἄκουσαν ἄκων· ἀλλ' ἐπηνάγκαζέ νιν
Διὸς χαλινὸς πρὸς βίαν πράσσειν τάδε.
εὐθὺς δὲ μορφὴ καὶ φρένες διάστροφοι
ἦσαν, κεραστὶς δ', ὡς ὁρᾶτ', ὀξυστόμῳ
μύωπι χρισθεῖσ' ἐμμανεῖ σκιρτήματι   675
ᾖσσον πρὸς εὔποτόν τε Κερχνείας ῥέος
ἀκτήν τε Λέρνης· βουκόλος δὲ γηγενὴς
ἄκρατος ὀργὴν Ἄργος ὡμάρτει, πυκνοῖς
ὄσσοις δεδορκὼς τοὺς ἐμοὺς κατὰ στίβους.
ἀπροσδόκητος δ' αὐτὸν ἀφνίδιος μόρος   680
τοῦ ζῆν ἀπεστέρησεν. οἰστροπλὴξ δ' ἐγὼ
μάστιγι θείᾳ γῆν πρὸ γῆς ἐλαύνομαι.
κλύεις τὰ πραχθέντ'· εἰ δ' ἔχεις εἰπεῖν ὅ τι
λοιπὸν πόνων, σήμαινε· μηδέ μ' οἰκτίσας
ξύνθαλπε μύθοις ψευδέσιν· νόσημα γὰρ   685
αἴσχιστον εἶναί φημι συνθέτους λόγους.
ΧΟ. ἔα ἔα, ἄπεχε, φεῦ·
οὔποτ' οὔποτ' ηὔχουν ξένους

μολεῖσθαι λόγους εἰς ἀκοὰν ἐμὰν,　690
οὐδ' ὧδε δυσθέατα καὶ δύσοιστα
πήματα, λύματα, δείματ' ἐμὰν
ἀμφάκει κέντρῳ ψήξειν ψυχάν·
ἰὼ ἰὼ μοῖρα μοῖρα,
πέφρικ' εἰσιδοῦσα πρᾶξιν Ἰοῦς.　695

ΠΡ.　πρό γε στενάζεις καὶ φόβου πλέα τις εἶ·
ἐπίσχες ἔς τ' ἂν καὶ τὰ λοιπὰ προσμάθῃς.

ΧΟ.　λέγ', ἐκδίδασκε· τοῖς νοσοῦσί τοι γλυκὺ
τὸ λοιπὸν ἄλγος προὐξεπίστασθαι τορῶς.

ΠΡ.　τὴν πρίν γε χρείαν ἠνύσασθ' ἐμοῦ πάρα　700
κούφως· μαθεῖν γὰρ τῆσδε πρῶτ' ἐχρήζετε
τὸν ἀμφ' ἑαυτῆς ἆθλον ἐξηγουμένης·
τὰ λοιπὰ νῦν ἀκούσαθ', οἷα χρὴ πάθη
τλῆναι πρὸς Ἥρας τήνδε τὴν νεάνιδα.
σύ τ', Ἰνάχειον σπέρμα, τοὺς ἐμοὺς λόγους　705
θυμῷ βάλ', ὡς ἂν τέρματ' ἐκμάθῃς ὁδοῦ.
πρῶτον μὲν ἐνθένδ' ἡλίου πρὸς ἀντολὰς
στρέψασα σαυτὴν στεῖχ' ἀνηρότους γύας·
Σκύθας δ' ἀφίξει νομάδας, οἳ πλεκτὰς στέγας
πεδάρσιοι ναίουσ' ἐπ' εὐκύκλοις ὄχοις,　710
ἐκηβόλοις· τόξοισιν ἐξηρτυμένοι·
οἷς μὴ πελάζειν, ἀλλ' ἁλιστόνοις πόδας
χρίμπτουσα ῥαχίαισιν ἐκπερᾶν χθόνα.
λαιᾶς δὲ χειρὸς οἱ σιδηροτέκτονες
οἰκοῦσι Χάλυβες, οὓς φυλάξασθαί σε χρή.　715
ἀνήμεροι γὰρ οὐδὲ πρόσπλατοι ξένοις.
ἥξεις δ' ὑβριστὴν ποταμὸν οὐ ψευδώνυμον,
ὃν μὴ περάσῃς, οὐ γὰρ εὔβατος περᾶν,
πρὶν ἂν πρὸς αὐτὸν Καύκασον μόλῃς, ὀρῶν
ὕψιστον, ἔνθα ποταμὸς ἐκφυσᾷ μένος　720
κροτάφων ἀπ' αὐτῶν. ἀστρογείτονας δὲ χρὴ

κορυφὰς ὑπερβάλλουσαν ἐς μεσημβρινὴν
βῆναι κέλευθον, ἔνθ' Ἀμαζόνων στρατὸν
ἥξει στυγάνορ', αἳ Θεμίσκυράν ποτε
κατοικιοῦσιν ἀμφὶ Θερμώδονθ', ἵνα   725
τραχεῖα πόντου Σαλμυδησία γνάθος
ἐχθρόξενος ναύταισι, μητρυιὰ νεῶν·
αὗταί σ' ὁδηγήσουσι καὶ μάλ' ἀσμένως.
ἰσθμὸν δ' ἐπ' αὐταῖς στενοπόροις λίμνης πύλαις
Κιμμερικὸν ἥξεις, ὃν θρασυσπλάγχνως σε χρὴ   730
λιποῦσαν αὐλῶν' ἐκπερᾶν Μαιωτικόν·
ἔσται δὲ θνητοῖς εἰσαεὶ λόγος μέγας
τῆς σῆς πορείας, Βόσπορος δ' ἐπώνυμος
κεκλήσεται. λιποῦσα δ' Εὐρώπης πέδον,
ἤπειρον ἥξεις Ἀσιάδ'. ἆρ' ὑμῖν δοκεῖ   735
ὁ τῶν θεῶν τύραννος ἐς τὰ πάνθ' ὁμῶς
βίαιος εἶναι; τῇδε γὰρ θνητῇ θεὸς
χρῄζων μιγῆναι τάσδ' ἐπέρριψεν πλάνας.
πικροῦ δ' ἔκυρσας, ὦ κόρη, τῶν σῶν γάμων
μνηστῆρος. οὓς γὰρ νῦν ἀκήκοας λόγους,   740
εἶναι δόκει σοὶ μηδέπω ἐν προοιμίοις.

ΙΩ.   ἰώ μοί μοι.

ΠΡ.   σὺ δ' αὖ κέκραγας κἀναμυχθίζει· τί που
      δράσεις, ὅταν τὰ λοιπὰ πυνθάνῃ κακά;

ΧΟ.   ἦ γάρ τι λοιπὸν τῇδε πημάτων ἐρεῖς;   745

ΠΡ.   δυσχείμερόν γε πέλαγος ἀτηρᾶς δύης.

ΙΩ.   τί δῆτ' ἐμοὶ ζῆν κέρδος, ἀλλ' οὐκ ἐν τάχει
      ἔρριψ' ἐμαυτὴν τῆσδ' ἀπὸ στύφλου πέτρας,
      ὅπως πέδοι σκήψασα τῶν πάντων πόνων
      ἀπηλλάγην; κρεῖσσον γὰρ εἰσάπαξ θανεῖν   750
      ἢ τὰς ἁπάσας ἡμέρας πάσχειν κακῶς.

ΠΡ.   ἦ δυσπετῶς ἂν τοὺς ἐμοὺς ἄθλους φέροις,
      ὅτῳ θανεῖν μέν ἐστιν οὐ πεπρωμένον·

αὕτη γὰρ ἦν ἂν πημάτων ἀπαλλαγή·
νῦν δ᾽ οὐδέν ἐστι τέρμα μοι προκείμενον   755
μόχθων, πρὶν ἂν Ζεὺς ἐκπέσῃ τυραννίδος.
ΙΩ. ἦ γάρ ποτ᾽ ἔστιν ἐκπεσεῖν ἀρχῆς Δία;
ΠΡ. ἥδοι᾽ ἂν, οἶμαι, τήνδ᾽ ἰδοῦσα συμφοράν.
ΙΩ. πῶς δ᾽ οὐκ ἂν, ἥτις ἐκ Διὸς πάσχω κακῶς;
ΠΡ. ὡς τοίνυν ὄντων τῶνδέ σοι μαθεῖν πάρα.   760
ΙΩ. πρὸς τοῦ τύραννα σκῆπτρα συληθήσεται;
ΠΡ. αὐτὸς πρὸς αὑτοῦ κενοφρόνων βουλευμάτων.
ΙΩ. ποίῳ τρόπῳ; σήμηνον, εἰ μή τις βλάβη.
ΠΡ. γαμεῖ γάμον τοιοῦτον ᾧ ποτ᾽ ἀσχαλᾷ.
ΙΩ. θέορτον, ἢ βρότειον; εἰ ῥητὸν, φράσον.   765
ΠΡ. τί δ᾽ ὅντιν᾽; οὐ γὰρ ῥητὸν αὐδᾶσθαι τόδε.
ΙΩ. ἦ πρὸς δάμαρτος ἐξανίσταται θρόνων;
ΠΡ. ἦ τέξεταί γε παῖδα φέρτερον πατρός.
ΙΩ. οὐδ᾽ ἔστιν αὐτῷ τῆσδ᾽ ἀποστροφὴ τύχης;
ΠΡ. οὐ δῆτα, πλὴν ἔγωγ᾽ ἂν ἐκ δεσμῶν λυθείς.   770
ΙΩ. τίς οὖν ὁ λύσων σ᾽ ἐστὶν ἄκοντος Διός;
ΠΡ. τῶν σῶν τιν᾽ αὐτὸν ἐκγόνων εἶναι χρεών.
ΙΩ. πῶς εἶπας; ἦ 'μὸς παῖς σ᾽ ἀπαλλάξει κακῶν;
ΠΡ. τρίτος γε γένναν πρὸς δέκ᾽ ἄλλαισιν γοναῖς.
ΙΩ. ἥδ᾽ οὐκέτ᾽ εὐξύμβλητος ἡ χρησμῳδία.   775
ΠΡ. καὶ μή τι σαυτῆς ἐκμαθεῖν ζήτει πόνους.
ΙΩ. μή μοι προτείνων κέρδος εἶτ᾽ ἀποστέρει.
ΠΡ. δυοῖν λόγοιν σε θατέρῳ δωρήσομαι.
ΙΩ. ποίοιν; πρόδειξον αἵρεσίν τ᾽ ἐμοὶ δίδου.
ΠΡ. δίδωμ᾽· ἑλοῦ γὰρ, ἢ πόνων τὰ λοιπά σοι   780
     φράσω σαφηνῶς, ἢ τὸν ἐκλύσοντ᾽ ἐμέ.
ΧΟ. τούτων σὺ τὴν μὲν τῇδε, τὴν δ᾽ ἐμοὶ χάριν
     θέσθαι θέλησον, μηδ᾽ ἀτιμάσῃς λόγου·
     καὶ τῇδε μὲν γέγωνε τὴν λοιπὴν πλάνην,
     ἐμοὶ δὲ τὸν λύσοντα· τοῦτο γὰρ ποθῶ.   785

ΠΡ. ἐπεὶ προθυμεῖσθ', οὐκ ἐναντιώσομαι
τὸ μὴ οὐ γεγωνεῖν πᾶν ὅσον προσχρῄζετε.
σοὶ πρῶτον, Ἰοῖ, πολύδονον πλάνην φράσω,
ἣν ἐγγράφου σὺ μνήμοσιν δέλτοις φρενῶν.
ὅταν περάσῃς ῥεῖθρον ἠπείρων ὅρον,   790
πρὸς ἀντολὰς φλογῶπας ἡλιοστιβεῖς
*   *   *   *   *   *
πόντου περῶσα φλοῖσβον, ἔς τ' ἂν ἐξίκῃ
πρὸς Γοργόνεια πεδία Κισθήνης, ἵνα
αἱ Φορκίδες ναίουσι δηναιαὶ κόραι
τρεῖς κυκνόμορφοι, κοινὸν ὄμμ' ἐκτημέναι,   795
μονόδοντες, ἃς οὔθ' ἥλιος προσδέρκεται
ἀκτῖσιν οὔθ' ἡ νύκτερος μήνη ποτέ.
πέλας δ' ἀδελφαὶ τῶνδε τρεῖς κατάπτεροι,
δρακοντόμαλλοι Γοργόνες βροτοστυγεῖς,
ἃς θνητὸς οὐδεὶς εἰσιδὼν ἕξει πνοάς·   800
τοιοῦτο μέν σοι τοῦτο φρούριον λέγω.
ἄλλην δ' ἄκουσον δυσχερῆ θεωρίαν·
ὀξυστόμους γὰρ Ζηνὸς ἀκραγεῖς κύνας
γρῦπας φύλαξαι, τόν τε μουνῶπα στρατὸν
Ἀριμασπὸν ἱπποβάμον', οἳ χρυσόρρυτον   805
οἰκοῦσιν ἀμφὶ νᾶμα Πλούτωνος πόρου·
τούτοις σὺ μὴ πέλαζε. τηλουρὸν δὲ γῆν
ἥξεις κελαινὸν φῦλον, οἳ πρὸς ἡλίου
ναίουσι πηγαῖς, ἔνθα ποταμὸς Αἰθίοψ.
τούτου παρ' ὄχθας ἕρφ', ἕως ἂν ἐξίκῃ   810
καταβασμὸν, ἔνθα Βυβλίνων ὀρῶν ἄπο
ἵησι σεπτὸν Νεῖλος εὔποτον ῥέος.
οὗτός σ' ὁδώσει τὴν τρίγωνον ἐς χθόνα
Νειλῶτιν, οὗ δὴ τὴν μακρὰν ἀποικίαν,
Ἰοῖ, πέπρωται σοί τε καὶ τέκνοις κτίσαι.   815
τῶν δ' εἴ τί σοι ψελλόν τε καὶ δυσεύρετον,

ἐπανδίπλαζε, καὶ σαφῶς ἐκμάνθανε·
σχολὴ δὲ πλείων ἢ θέλω πάρεστί μοι.

ΧΟ. εἰ μέν τι τῇδε λοιπὸν ἢ παρειμένον
ἔχεις γεγωνεῖν τῆς πολυφθόρου πλάνης,　82ϑ
λέγ'· εἰ δὲ πάντ' εἴρηκας, ἡμῖν αὖ χάριν
δὸς ἥντιν' αἰτούμεσθα, μέμνησαι δέ που.

ΠΡ. τὸ πᾶν πορείας ἥδε τέρμ' ἀκήκοεν.
ὅπως δ' ἂν εἰδῇ μὴ μάτην κλύουσά μου,
ἃ πρὶν μολεῖν δεῦρ' ἐκμεμόχθηκεν φράσω,　825
τεκμήριον τοῦτ' αὐτὸ δοὺς μύθων ἐμῶν.
ὄχλον μὲν οὖν τὸν πλεῖστον ἐκλείψω λόγων,
πρὸς αὐτὸ δ' εἶμι τέρμα σῶν πλανημάτων.
ἐπεὶ γὰρ ἦλθες πρὸς Μολοσσὰ γάπεδα,
τὴν αἰπύνωτόν τ' ἀμφὶ Δωδώνην, ἵνα　830
μαντεῖα θᾶκός τ' ἐστὶ Θεσπρωτοῦ Διός,
τέρας τ' ἄπιστον, αἱ προσήγοροι δρύες,
ὑφ' ὧν σὺ λαμπρῶς κοὐδὲν αἰνικτηρίως
προσηγορεύθης ἡ Διὸς κλεινὴ δάμαρ
[μέλλουσ' ἔσεσθαι, τῶνδε προσσαίνει σέ τι].　835
ἐντεῦθεν οἰστρήσασα ἣν παρακτίαν
κέλευθον ᾖξας πρὸς μέγαν κόλπον 'Ρέας,
ἀφ' οὗ παλιμπλάγκτοισι χειμάζει δρόμοις·
χρόνον δὲ τὸν μέλλοντα πόντιος μυχὸς,
σαφῶς ἐπίστασ', 'Ιόνιος κεκλήσεται,　840
τῆς σῆς πορείας μνῆμα τοῖς πᾶσιν βροτοῖς.
σημεῖά σοι τάδ' ἐστὶ τῆς ἐμῆς φρενὸς,
ὡς δέρκεται πλέον τι τοῦ πεφασμένου.
τὰ λοιπὰ δ' ὑμῖν τῇδέ τ' ἐς κοινὸν φράσω,
ἐς ταυτὸν ἐλθὼν τῶν πάλαι λόγων ἴχνος.　845
ἔστιν πόλις Κάνωβος ἐσχάτη χθονὸς,
Νείλου πρὸς αὐτῷ στόματι καὶ προσχώματι·
ἐνταῦθα δή σε Ζεὺς τίθησιν ἔμφρονα,

ἐπαφῶν ἀταρβεῖ χειρὶ καὶ θιγὼν μόνον.
ἐπώνυμον δὲ τῶν Διὸς γεννημάτων   850
τέξεις κελαινὸν Ἔπαφον, ὃς καρπώσεται
ὅσην πλατύρρους Νεῖλος ἀρδεύει χθόνα·
πέμπτη δ᾽ ἀπ᾽ αὐτοῦ γέννα πεντηκοντάπαις
πάλιν πρὸς Ἄργος οὐχ ἑκοῦσ᾽ ἐλεύσεται
θηλύσπορος, φεύγουσα συγγενῆ γάμον   855
ἀνεψιῶν· οἱ δ᾽ ἐπτοημένοι φρένας,
κίρκοι πελειῶν οὐ μακρὰν λελειμμένοι,
ἥξουσι θηρεύοντες οὐ θηρασίμους
γάμους, φθόνον δὲ σωμάτων ἕξει θεός·
Πελασγία δὲ δέξεται θηλυκτόνῳ   860
Ἄρει δαμέντων νυκτιφρουρήτῳ θράσει·
γυνὴ γὰρ ἄνδρ᾽ ἕκαστον αἰῶνος στερεῖ,
δίθηκτον ἐν σφαγαῖσι βάψασα ξίφος·
τοιάδ᾽ ἐπ᾽ ἐχθροὺς τοὺς ἐμοὺς ἔλθοι Κύπρις.
μίαν δὲ παίδων ἵμερος θέλξει τὸ μὴ   865
κτεῖναι ξύνευνον, ἀλλ᾽ ἀπαμβλυνθήσεται
γνώμην· δυοῖν δὲ θάτερον βουλήσεται,
κλύειν ἄναλκις μᾶλλον ἢ μιαιφόνος·
αὕτη κατ᾽ Ἄργος βασιλικὸν τέξει γένος.
μακροῦ λόγου δεῖ ταῦτ᾽ ἐπεξελθεῖν τορῶς.   870
σπορᾶς γε μὴν ἐκ τῆσδε φύσεται θρασὺς
τόξοισι κλεινός, ὃς πόνων ἐκ τῶνδ᾽ ἐμὲ
λύσει. τοιόνδε χρησμὸν ἡ παλαιγενὴς
μήτηρ ἐμοὶ διῆλθε Τιτανὶς Θέμις·
ὅπως δὲ χὤπῃ, ταῦτα δεῖ μακροῦ χρόνου   875
εἰπεῖν, σύ τ᾽ οὐδὲν ἐκμαθοῦσα κερδανεῖς.

ΙΩ. ἐλελεῦ ἐλελεῦ, ὑπό μ᾽ αὖ σφάκελος
καὶ φρενοπληγεῖς μανίαι θάλπουσ᾽,
οἴστρου δ᾽ ἄρδις χρίει μ᾽ ἄπυρος·   880
κραδία δὲ φόβῳ φρένα λακτίζει.

τροχοδινεῖται δ' ὄμμαθ' ἑλίγδην,
ἔξω δὲ δρόμου φέρομαι λύσσης
πνεύματι μάργῳ, γλώσσης ἀκρατής·
θολεροὶ δὲ λόγοι παίουσ' εἰκῇ   885
στυγνῆς πρὸς κύμασιν ἄτης.

ΧΟ. ἦ σοφὸς ἦ σοφὸς ὃς   στρ. α'
πρῶτος ἐν γνώμᾳ τόδ' ἐβάστασε καὶ γλώσσᾳ
     διεμυθολόγησεν,
ὡς τὸ κηδεῦσαι καθ' ἑαυτὸν ἀριστεύει μακρῷ,   890
καὶ μήτε τῶν πλούτῳ διαθρυπτομένων
μήτε τῶν γέννᾳ μεγαλυνομένων
ὄντα χερνήταν ἐραστεῦσαι γάμων.
μήποτε μήποτέ μ', ὦ   ἀντ. α'
πότνιαι Μοῖραι, λεχέων Διὸς εὐνάτειραν ἴδοισθε
     πέλουσαν·   895
μηδὲ πλαθείην γαμέτᾳ τινὶ τῶν ἐξ οὐρανοῦ.
ταρβῶ γὰρ ἀστεργάνορα παρθενίαν
εἰσορῶσ' Ἰοῦς μέγα δαπτομέναν
δυσπλάνοις Ἥρας ἀλατείαις πόνων.   900
ἐμοὶ δ' ὅτι μὲν ὁμαλὸς ὁ γάμος
οὐ δέδια, μηδὲ κρεισσόνων
θεῶν ἄφυκτον ὄμμα προσδράκοι με.
ἀπολέμιστος ὅδε γ' ὁ πόλεμος, ἄπορα πόριμος,
οὐδ' ἔχω τίς ἂν γενοίμαν· Διὸς γὰρ οὐχ ὁρῶ   905
μῆτιν ὅπα φύγοιμ' ἄν.

ΠΡ. ἦ μὴν ἔτι Ζεὺς, καίπερ αὐθάδη φρονῶν,
ἔσται ταπεινός· τοῖον ἐξαρτύεται
γάμον γαμεῖν, ὃς αὐτὸν ἐκ τυραννίδος
θρόνων τ' ἄϊστον ἐκβαλεῖ· πατρὸς δ' ἀρὰ   910
Κρόνου τότ' ἤδη παντελῶς κρανθήσεται,
ἣν ἐκπίτνων ἠρᾶτο δηναιῶν θρόνων.
τοιῶνδε μόχθων ἐκτροπὴν οὐδεὶς θεῶν

δύναιτ' ἂν αὐτῷ πλὴν ἐμοῦ δεῖξαι σαφῶς.
ἐγὼ τάδ' οἶδα χὢ τρόπῳ· πρὸς ταῦτά νυν   915
θαρσῶν καθήσθω τοῖς πεδαρσίοις κτύποις
πιστὸς, τινάσσων τ' ἐν χεροῖν πύρπνουν βέλος.
οὐδὲν γὰρ αὐτῷ ταῦτ' ἐπαρκέσει τὸ μὴ οὐ
πεσεῖν ἀτίμως πτώματ' οὐκ ἀνασχετά·
τοῖον παλαιστὴν νῦν παρασκευάζεται   920
ἐπ' αὐτὸς αὑτῷ, δυσμαχώτατον τέρας·
ὃς δὴ κεραυνοῦ κρεῖσσον εὑρήσει φλόγα,
βροντάς θ' ὑπερβάλλοντα καρτερὸν κτύπον·
θαλασσίαν τε γῆς τινάκτειραν νόσον
τρίαιναν, αἰχμὴν τὴν Ποσειδῶνος, σκεδᾷ.   925
πταίσας δὲ τῷδε πρὸς κακῷ μαθήσεται
ὅσον τό τ' ἄρχειν καὶ τὸ δουλεύειν δίχα.
ΧΟ. σύ θην ἃ χρῄζεις, ταῦτ' ἐπιγλωσσᾷ Διός.
ΠΡ. ἅπερ τελεῖται, πρὸς δ' ἃ βούλομαι λέγω.
ΧΟ. καὶ προσδοκᾶν χρὴ δεσπόσειν Διός τινα;   930
ΠΡ. καὶ τῶνδέ γ' ἕξει δυσλοφωτέρους πόνους.
ΧΟ. πῶς δ' οὐχὶ ταρβεῖς τοιάδ' ἐκρίπτων ἔπη;
ΠΡ. τί δ' ἂν φοβοίμην ᾧ θανεῖν οὐ μόρσιμον;
ΧΟ. ἀλλ' ἆθλον ἄν σοι τοῦδ' ἔτ' ἀλγίω πόροι.
ΠΡ. ὁ δ' οὖν ποιείτω· πάντα προσδοκητά μοι.   935
ΧΟ. οἱ προσκυνοῦντες τὴν Ἀδράστειαν σοφοί.
ΠΡ. σέβου, προσεύχου, θῶπτε τὸν κρατοῦντ' ἀεί.
ἐμοὶ δ' ἔλασσού Ζηνὸς ἢ μηδὲν μέλει.
δράτω, κρατείτω τόνδε τὸν βραχὺν χρόνον,
ὅπως θέλει· δαρὸν γὰρ οὐκ ἄρξει θεοῖς.   940
ἀλλ' εἰσορῶ γὰρ τόνδε τὸν Διὸς τρόχιν,
τὸν τοῦ τυράννου τοῦ νέου διάκονον·
πάντως τι καινὸν ἀγγελῶν ἐλήλυθε.

ΕΡΜΗΣ.

σὲ τὸν σοφιστὴν, τὸν πικρῶς ὑπέρπικρον,
τὸν ἐξαμαρτόντ' ἐς θεοὺς ἐφημέροις   945
πορόντα τιμὰς, τὸν πυρὸς κλέπτην λέγω·
πατὴρ ἄνωγέ σ' οὕστινας κομπεῖς γάμους
αὐδᾶν, πρὸς ὧν ἐκεῖνος ἐκπίπτει κράτους·
καὶ ταῦτα μέντοι μηδὲν αἰνικτηρίως,
ἀλλ' αὔθ' ἕκαστ' ἔκφραζε· μηδέ μοι διπλᾶς   950
ὁδοὺς, Προμηθεῦ, προσβάλῃς· ὁρᾷς δ' ὅτι
Ζεὺς τοῖς τοιούτοις οὐχὶ μαλθακίζεται.

ΠΡ. σεμνόστομός γε καὶ φρονήματος πλέως
ὁ μῦθός ἐστιν, ὡς θεῶν ὑπηρέτου.

· νέον νέοι κρατεῖτε καὶ δοκεῖτε δὴ   955
ναίειν ἀπενθῆ πέργαμ'· οὐκ ἐκ τῶνδ' ἐγὼ
δισσοὺς τυράννους ἐκπεσόντας ᾐσθόμην;
τρίτον δὲ τὸν νῦν κοιρανοῦντ' ἐπόψομαι
αἴσχιστα καὶ τάχιστα. μή τί σοι δοκῶ
ταρβεῖν ὑποπτήσσειν τε τοὺς νέους θεούς;   960
πολλοῦ γε καὶ τοῦ παντὸς ἐλλείπω. σὺ δὲ
κέλευθον ἥνπερ ἦλθες ἐγκόνει πάλιν·
πεύσει γὰρ οὐδὲν ὧν ἀνιστορεῖς ἐμέ.

ΕΡ. τοιοῖσδε μέντοι καὶ πρὶν αὐθαδίσμασιν
ἐς τάσδε σαυτὸν πημονὰς καθώρμισας.   965

ΠΡ. τῆς σῆς λατρείας τὴν ἐμὴν δυσπραξίαν,
σαφῶς ἐπίστασ', οὐκ ἂν ἀλλάξαιμ' ἐγώ.
κρεῖσσον γὰρ οἶμαι τῇδε λατρεύειν πέτρᾳ
ἢ πατρὶ φῦναι Ζηνὶ πιστὸν ἄγγελον.
οὕτως ὑβρίζειν τοὺς ὑβρίζοντας χρεών.   970

ΕΡ. χλιδᾶν ἔοικας τοῖς παροῦσι πράγμασι.

ΠΡ. χλιδῶ; χλιδῶντας ὧδε τοὺς ἐμοὺς ἐγὼ
ἐχθροὺς ἴδοιμι· καὶ σὲ δ' ἐν τούτοις λέγω.

D

ΕΡ. ἦ κἀμὲ γάρ τι ξυμφοραῖς ἐπαιτιᾷ ;
ΠΡ. ἁπλῷ λόγῳ τοὺς πάντας ἐχθαίρω θεούς,   975
    ὅσοι παθόντες εὖ κακοῦσί μ' ἐκδίκως.
ΕΡ. κλύω σ' ἐγὼ μεμηνότ' οὐ σμικρὰν νόσον.
ΠΡ. νοσοῖμ' ἂν, εἰ νόσημα τοὺς ἐχθροὺς στυγεῖν.
ΕΡ. εἴης φορητὸς οὐκ ἂν, εἰ πράσσοις καλῶς.
ΠΡ. ὤμοι.   ΕΡ. τόδε Ζεὺς τοὔπος οὐκ ἐπίσταται.   980
ΠΡ. ἀλλ' ἐκδιδάσκει πάνθ' ὁ γηράσκων χρόνος.
ΕΡ. καὶ μὴν σύ γ' οὔπω σωφρονεῖν ἐπίστασαι.
ΠΡ. σὲ γὰρ προσηύδων οὐκ ἂν ὄνθ' ὑπηρέτην.
ΕΡ. ἐρεῖν ἔοικας οὐδὲν ὧν χρῄζει πατήρ.
ΠΡ. καὶ μὴν ὀφείλων γ' ἂν τίνοιμ' αὐτῷ χάριν.   985
ΕΡ. ἐκερτόμησας δῆθεν ὡς παῖδ' ὄντα με.
ΠΡ. οὐ γὰρ σὺ παῖς τε κἄτι τοῦδ' ἀνούστερος,
    εἰ προσδοκᾷς ἐμοῦ τι πεύσεσθαι πάρα ;
    οὐκ ἔστιν αἴκισμ' οὐδὲ μηχάνημ' ὅτῳ
    προτρέψεταί με Ζεὺς γεγωνῆσαι τάδε,   990
    πρὶν ἂν χαλασθῇ δεσμὰ λυμαντήρια.
    πρὸς ταῦτα ῥιπτέσθω μὲν αἰθαλοῦσσα φλόξ,
    λευκοπτέρῳ δὲ νιφάδι καὶ βροντήμασι
    χθονίοις κυκάτω πάντα καὶ ταρασσέτω·
    γνάμψει γὰρ οὐδὲν τῶνδέ μ' ὥστε καὶ φράσαι   995
    πρὸς οὗ χρεών νιν ἐκπεσεῖν τυραννίδος.
ΕΡ. ὅρα νυν εἴ σοι ταῦτ' ἀρωγὰ φαίνεται.
ΠΡ. ὦπται πάλαι δὴ καὶ βεβούλευται τάδε.
ΕΡ. τόλμησον, ὦ μάταιε, τόλμησόν ποτε
    πρὸς τὰς παρούσας πημονὰς ὀρθῶς φρονεῖν.   1000
ΠΡ. ὀχλεῖς μάτην με κῦμ' ὅπως παρηγορῶν.
    εἰσελθέτω σε μήποθ' ὡς ἐγὼ Διὸς
    γνώμην φοβηθεὶς θηλύνους γενήσομαι
    καὶ λιπαρήσω τὸν μέγα στυγούμενον
    γυναικομίμοις ὑπτιάσμασιν χερῶν   1005

λῦσαί με δεσμῶν τῶνδε· τοῦ παντὸς δέω.

ΕΡ. λέγων ἔοικα πολλὰ καὶ μάτην ἐρεῖν·
τέγγει γὰρ οὐδὲν οὐδὲ μαλθάσσει κέαρ
λιταῖς· δακὼν δὲ στόμιον ὡς νεοζυγὴς
πῶλος βιάζει καὶ πρὸς ἡνίας μάχει.   1010
ἀτὰρ σφοδρύνει γ᾽ ἀσθενεῖ σοφίσματι.
αὐθαδία γὰρ τῷ φρονοῦντι μὴ καλῶς
αὐτὴ καθ᾽ αὑτὴν οὐδενὸς μεῖον σθένει.
σκέψαι δ᾽, ἐὰν μὴ τοῖς ἐμοῖς πεισθῇς λόγοις,
οἷός σε χειμὼν·καὶ κακῶν τρικυμία   1015
ἔπεισ᾽ ἄφυκτος· πρῶτα μὲν γὰρ ὀκρίδα
φάραγγα βροντῇ καὶ κεραυνίᾳ φλογὶ
πατὴρ σπαράξει τήνδε, καὶ κρύψει δέμας
τὸ σὸν, πετραία δ᾽ ἀγκάλη σε βαστάσει.
μακρὸν δὲ μῆκος ἐκτελευτήσας χρόνου   1020
ἄψορρον ἥξεις ἐς φάος· Διὸς δέ τοι
πτηνὸς κύων, δαφοινὸς ἀετός, λάβρως
διαρταμήσει σώματος μέγα ῥάκος,
ἄκλητος ἕρπων δαιταλεὺς πανήμερος,
κελαινόβρωτον δ᾽ ἧπαρ ἐκθοινήσεται.   1025
τοιοῦδε μόχθου τέρμα μή τι προσδόκα,
πρὶν ἂν θεῶν τις διάδοχος τῶν σῶν πόνων
φανῇ, θελήσῃ τ᾽ εἰς ἀναύγητον μολεῖν
Ἅιδην κνεφαῖά τ᾽ ἀμφὶ Ταρτάρου βάθη.
πρὸς ταῦτα βούλευ᾽· ὡς ὅδ᾽ οὐ πεπλασμένος   1030
ὁ κόμπος, ἀλλὰ καὶ λίαν εἰρημένος·
ψευδηγορεῖν γὰρ οὐκ ἐπίσταται στόμα
τὸ Δῖον, ἀλλὰ πᾶν ἔπος τελεῖ. σὺ δὲ
πάπταινε καὶ φρόντιζε, μηδ᾽ αὐθαδίαν
εὐβουλίας ἀμείνον᾽ ἡγήσῃ ποτέ.   1035

ΧΟ. ἡμῖν μὲν Ἑρμῆς οὐκ ἄκαιρα φαίνεται
λέγειν· ἄνωγε γάρ σε τὴν αὐθαδίαν

D 2

μεθέντ' ἐρευνᾶν τὴν σοφὴν εὐβουλίαν.
πιθοῦ· σοφῷ γὰρ αἰσχρὸν ἐξαμαρτάνειν.

ΠΡ. εἰδότι τοί μοι τάσδ' ἀγγελίας   1040
ὅδ' ἐθώϋξεν, πάσχειν δὲ κακῶς
ἐχθρὸν ὑπ' ἐχθρῶν οὐδὲν ἀεικές.
πρὸς ταῦτ' ἐπ' ἐμοὶ ῥιπτέσθω μὲν
πυρὸς ἀμφήκης βόστρυχος, αἰθὴρ δ'
ἐρεθιζέσθω   1045
βροντῇ σφακέλῳ τ' ἀγρίων ἀνέμων·
χθόνα δ' ἐκ πυθμένων αὐταῖς ῥίζαις
πνεῦμα κραδαίνοι,
κῦμα δὲ πόντου τραχεῖ ῥοθίῳ
ξυγχώσειεν τῶν τ' οὐρανίων
ἄστρων διόδους, ἔς τε κελαινὸν   1050
Τάρταρον ἄρδην ῥίψειε δέμας
τοὐμὸν ἀνάγκης στερραῖς δίναις·
πάντως ἐμέ γ' οὐ θανατώσει.

ΕΡ. τοιάδε μέντοι τῶν φρενοπλήκτων
βουλεύματ' ἔπη τ' ἐστὶν ἀκοῦσαι.   1055
τί γὰρ ἐλλείπει μὴ παραπαίειν
ἢ τοῦδε τύχη; τί χαλᾷ μανιῶν;
ἀλλ' οὖν ὑμεῖς γ' αἱ πημοσύναις
ξυγκάμνουσαι ταῖς τοῦδε τόπων
μετά ποι χωρεῖτ' ἐκ τῶνδε θοῶς,   1060
μὴ φρένας ὑμῶν ἠλιθιώσῃ
βροντῆς μύκημ' ἀτέραμνον.

ΧΟ. ἄλλο τι φώνει καὶ παραμυθοῦ μ'
ὅ τι καὶ πείσεις· οὐ γὰρ δή που
τοῦτό γε τλητὸν παρέσυρας ἔπος.   1065
πῶς με κελεύεις κακότητ' ἀσκεῖν;
μετὰ τοῦδ' ὅ τι χρὴ πάσχειν ἐθέλω·
τοὺς προδότας γὰρ μισεῖν ἔμαθον,

κοὐκ ἔστι νόσος
τῆσδ' ἥντιν' ἀπέπτυσα μᾶλλον.　　　　1070

ΕΡ. ἀλλ' οὖν μέμνησθ' ἁγὼ προλέγω·
μηδὲ πρὸς ἄτης θηραθεῖσαι
μέμψησθε τύχην, μηδέ ποτ' εἴπηθ'
ὡς Ζεὺς ὑμᾶς εἰς ἀπρόοπτον
πῆμ' εἰσέβαλεν·　　　　　　　　　1075
μὴ δῆτ', αὐταὶ δ' ὑμᾶς αὐτάς.
εἰδυῖαι γὰρ κοὐκ ἐξαίφνης
οὐδὲ λαθραίως
εἰς ἀπέραντον δίκτυον ἄτης
ἐμπλεχθήσεσθ' ὑπ' ἀνοίας.

ΠΡ. καὶ μὴν ἔργῳ κοὐκέτι μύθῳ　　　1080
χθὼν σεσάλευται·
βρυχία δ' ἠχὼ παραμυκᾶται
βροντῆς, ἕλικες δ' ἐκλάμπουσι
στεροπῆς ζάπυροι,
στρόμβοι δὲ κόνιν εἱλίσσουσι·　　　1085
σκιρτᾷ δ' ἀνέμων πνεύματα πάντων
εἰς ἄλληλα
στάσιν ἀντίπνουν ἀποδεικνύμενα·
ξυντετάρακται δ' αἰθὴρ πόντῳ.
τοιάδ' ἐπ' ἐμοὶ ῥιπὴ Διόθεν
τεύχουσα φόβον στείχει φανερῶς.　　1090
ὦ μητρὸς ἐμῆς σέβας, ὦ πάντων
αἰθὴρ κοινὸν φάος εἱλίσσων,
ἐσορᾷς μ' ὡς ἔκδικα πάσχω.

NOTES.

Line 1. ἥκομεν. The verb is perfect in sense, and, standing at the beginning of a play, shows the exact point which the action has already reached. Cp. Euripides, Hecuba, 1, ἥκω, νεκρῶν κευθμῶνα καὶ σκότου πύλας | λιπών.

l. 2. Σκύθην. See Introduction, p. ix. οἶμον, lit. 'a road' (probably from εἶμι). Hence a strip, as οἶμοι κυάνοιο (Hom. Il. 11. 24), strips or layers of tin. Here it is the tract, region of Scythia. Compare the use of the word in l. 394. We often find that Aeschylus, when he introduces a rare word, uses it more than once in the same play, either with the same or with a varied sense. All such cases should be noticed, and the passages compared. ἄβατον. See Appendix A.

l. 3. This line answers to l. 1. 'We (the whole party) have come to the appointed place, it remains for thee (Hephaestus) to do thine office.' δὲ does not directly answer to μὲν, but is used to introduce the clause following the vocative, as in Eur. Orest. 622, Μενέλαε, σοὶ δὲ τάδε λέγω κ. τ. λ. Very many Greek plays begin with a clause containing μὲν, which is sometimes followed by δὲ, sometimes by some other form of antithesis. σοὶ, dative after μέλειν.

l. 4. ἃς is practically a cognate accusative after ἐφεῖτο, as though it were ἐπιστολὰς ἅς σοι πατὴρ ἐπέστειλεν.

l. 5. ὀχμάσαι is epexegetical of ἐπιστολάς; that is, it explains the nature of the commands. For the verb see l. 618.

l. 6. This line, as it stands in the text, is, as to caesura and rhythm, characteristic of Aeschylus.

l. 7. The reason of the emphatic σοὶ in ll. 3-4: Hephaestus was the greatest loser by the theft of the fire, which placed in the power of mortals arts till then his alone. ἄνθος, the flower, or best, of everything. So χρημάτων ἄνθος (Agam. 954-5), the best of the spoil. Rarely with possessive genitive, or, as here, pronoun; the choicest thing thou hadst. παντέχνου, because so many arts depended on fire. See ll. 110 and 254.

l. 8. ὥπασεν. Cp. l. 30 and l. 252. τοιᾶσδέ τοι κ. τ. λ. 'Such was his offence, and for it he is now to pay forfeit to the gods.' τοιᾶσδε refers to what has preceded, and cannot be distinguished in use from τοιαῦτα in l. 28. τοι emphasises the statement. Prometheus' offence was really more comprehensive. See his own statement of it in l. 226, etc. and l. 436, etc.—But it suits the speaker's purpose to dwell on the special wrong done to the Fire-god.

l. 10. ἄν is frequently found in clauses which denote purpose (*final clauses*), inserted between the conjunction ὡς or ὅπως (never ἵνα) and the verb. By comparing other cases (see ll. 654, 706, 824) the exact meaning will be best caught. Here, had we found ὡς διδαχθῇ, the sense would be 'he is to be punished in order that he may be taught;' with ὡς ἂν διδαχθῇ it is 'he is to be punished that so by the best possible means (by an adequate punishment) he may be taught.' Observe the word τυραννίς, which is elsewhere used in a bad sense of Zeus' irresponsible rule (see l. 224, etc.), here employed 'cynically,' as we should say, by the agent of Zeus.

l. 11. στέργειν, 'to acquiesce in;' used in this sense with accusative, as here, or with dative, or absolutely, as in Soph. O. T. 11. φιλανθρώπου τρόπου, a brutal scoff at Prometheus' good will towards mankind. The words are repeated, but in a different tone, by Hephaestus (l. 28).

l. 12. σφῷν, dative of general reference (ethical dative). 'So far as you are concerned, the command of Zeus is quite fulfilled, and there is nothing to hinder me more;' that is, you have brought your prisoner here; what remains is for me to do, and with that you are not concerned. There is a dignity in Hephaestus' bearing towards the ministers of Zeus, which in the sequel we find him ill able to maintain. See ll. 36-81, and especially 72-3.

l. 13. ἐμποδών, sc. ἐστί μοι.

l. 14. ἄτολμός εἰμι = 'I have not the heart,' see l. 999. συγγενῆ θεόν, the relationship, here and in l. 39, must be understood in a general sense, for Hephaestus was a son of Zeus and Hera and therefore not closely akin to Prometheus.

l. 15. φάραγγι πρὸς δυσχειμέρῳ, 'up to this rocky cleft exposed to all foul weather.'

l. 16. 'Whether or no, I must needs get the heart.' Observe the genitive τῶνδε. σχεθεῖν, an aorist form, since no present σχέθω is known.

l. 17. ἐξωριάζειν, i. e. ἐξ ὥρας τιθέναι, 'to disregard.' The word is not known elsewhere. See Appendix A.

l. 18. As he turns to Prometheus, the language of Hephaestus is full of respect and sympathy, mingled with regretful wonder at thoughts which have proved too lofty to be safe. Compare this address with the intrusive sympathy of Ocean (1. 288, etc.), and with the gentle feminine comfort offered by the Chorus, and from them acceptable. See Soph. O. C. 1636 of Theseus approaching the suffering Oedipus, 'like a true knight, with no hint of pity,' (ὡς ἀνὴρ γενναῖος, οὐκ οἴκτου μέτα.) For the mother of Prometheus see on 1. 210.

1. 19. The repetition of words is frequent in Aeschylus, who takes the practice from Homer; and always has a special force. Here *mutual* unwillingness is meant. Compare ll. 29, 192, 671, etc. and see note on l. 276.

ll. 21, 2. This is a case of *zeugma*, the verb having to be taken with two substantives, though really appropriate only to the latter. The full sense would be given by ἵν' οὔτε φωνὴν ἀκούσει τινὸς βροτῶν οὔτε μορφὴν ὄψει.

l. 23. Often in Greek the real statement is made not by the verb, but by an adjective or participle; which may be, as here, in an oblique case. Cp. l. 277. 'Thou shalt joy to see night hide the daylight, and joy to see the sun return in his course.' Each change shall seem to offer relief from an ever intolerable present. Cp. Deut. xxix. 67, 'In the morning thou shalt say, "Would God it were even!" and at even thou shalt say, "Would God it were morning!"' The words of Hephaestus are no threat, but a regretful reflection.

l. 24. ποικιλείμων. So Sophocles speaks of αἰόλα νύξ (Trach. 94). The compound word is, in form, and in the image which it contains, characteristic of Aeschylus.

l. 27. The words οὐ πέφυκέ πω, 'hath not *yet* been born,' convey a hint, unconscious perhaps on Hephaestus' part, that a deliverer should one day be born, see ll. 771–2.

l. 28. τοιαῦτ' ἐπηύρου (ἐπαυρίσκομαι). 'Such the enjoyment thou didst win by thy fashion of benevolence.' Cp. l. 11.

l. 29. See note on l. 19.

l. 30. ὤπασας. See l. 8, and l. 252. πέρα δίκης. There is little or no condemnation of Prometheus' acts in these words. He had unquestionably passed bounds, and was to suffer for it, but those bounds might have been set by an arbitrary tyrant. Cp. Horace, Odes, I. 3. 27, 'Audax Iapeti genus | Ignem *fraude mala* gentibus obtulit.'

l. 31. ἀνθ' ὧν, 'in return for which conduct.' φρουρήσεις, 'like a sentry;' see on l. 218.

l. 32. κάμπτων γόνυ, i.e. in rest. Cp. l. 396.

l. 35. Zeus is throughout this play the upstart monarch, new to power and *therefore* harsh. In Agam. 1043, Cassandra, coming to Mycenae as a captive, is told that she should be thankful to belong to a family old in its inheritance, since those who reap unhoped for harvests of prosperity are always harsh and arbitrary.

l. 38. ὅστις is not the simple relative, like ὅς, but gives the reason why Prometheus ought to be hated. It would be rendered in Latin by *qui* with perfect subjunctive; so in l. 753, and l. 759. For its generalising force (with or without ἄν) see l. 35 and l. 243, for its use in a dependent question, l. 295, etc. τὸ σὸν γέρας, i.e. 'fire,' see l. 7. But see Appendix A.

l. 39. In the dialogue which follows, one line of Hephaestus' is in each case answered by two of Strength's. The demon is exultant and insolent, the God reluctant and dignified.   τὸ ξυγγενές τοι κ.τ.λ., 'relationship (see l. 14) is a strong tie, and the dealings too which we have had with one another,' (when they practised the smith's art together.) τοί has a *gnomic* force, that is, shows that Aeschylus is referring to, and half quoting, some well-known γνώμη or proverb. 'As they say, kin should be kind,' or the like; see ll. 275, 698. This is only a special variety of its use in emphasising words and statements, as in l. 8.

l. 41. οἷόν τε πῶς, 'how is it possible?' with infinitive as in l. 107. In l. 84 we have οἷοί τε personally, as often in Homer.   τοῦτο, i.e. 'disobedience.'

l. 42. Hephaestus gives in to the dilemma thus harshly stated, and states his reason for doing so to be his adversary's harshness. 'I might have known that you are always pitiless, and *therefore* it is no use arguing.' Cp. the use of γε in giving assent, as in l. 254.

l. 43. This would be in full: τὸ γὰρ θρηνεῖσθαι τόνδε οὐδέν ἐστιν ἄκος τῶν παθῶν αὐτοῦ.

l. 44. μὴ πόνει (present), 'do not go on labouring.' τὰ μηδὲν ὠφελοῦντα (cognate acc.), 'with useless efforts.'

l. 46. νιν, sc. τὴν χειρωναξίαν. ὡς ἁπλῷ λόγῳ (sc. φράσαι). ὡς is prefixed to many infinitives, as ὡς εἰπεῖν, ὡς εἰκάσαι, and ὡς τορῶς φράσαι (Agam. 1584). Compare its use with some adverbs, as ὡς ἀληθῶς.

l. 47. The argument is that Hephaestus is a mere instrument, and Prometheus may thank himself for his sufferings.

l. 48. ἔμπας (ἐν πᾶσι), 'for all that,' so often in Homer and Hesiod, sometimes with ἀλλά, as in l. 187. ὤφελεν conveys a wish, with or without such optative particles as εἴθε, ὡς.

l. 49. 'Everything has its burden, except to be ruler of the gods.' An answer to Hephaestus' wish that his present office had rather fallen to some one else; but see Appendix A. For the dative cp. l. 940, δαρὸν γὰρ οὐκ ἄρξει θεοῖς.

l. 50. This line well describes the condition of the subjects of a τυραννίς, and would be welcome, by contrast, to the citizens of free Athens.

l. 51. This would be in full ἔγνωκα τάδε καὶ τοῖσδε οὐδὲν ἀντειπεῖν ἔχω. καὶ is said to be *transposed*, that is, it follows, instead of preceding τοῖσδε. Probably it would be more correct to say that τοῖσδε is written instead of τάδε, the dative being due to ἀντειπεῖν in a distant part of the line. Compare the construction in l. 331.

l. 52. οὔκουν, with future indicative, is a strong command. Cp. l. 616.

l. 53. ἐλινύοντα, see l. 530. Strength, relying on Zeus' commission, uses the tone which he knows will be most provoking to Hephaestus. Zeus, as in l. 312, and l. 947, is represented as the τύραννος who sits far away in his palace, but sees and hears, himself or through spies, all which passes in his dominions.

l. 54. καὶ δή, 'look! the shackles are ready, thou mayest see them.' καὶ δή is often used when something is presented to the eyes, especially in rejoinders : see l. 75.

l. 55. νιν, Prometheus. Hephaestus is directed to seize both the hands of Prometheus, binding them together (as with handcuffs), and with the hammer to drive into the rock the nails which are to secure the chain binding hands and arms. There does not seem to be any idea of extended arms, as in the Roman punishment of the cross.

l. 57. περαίνεται δή, 'it is being completed, do you not see?' δή of indignant emphasis.

l. 59. 'For he has a strange power of finding a way even out of a desperate plight.' Cp. l. 111. See Appendix A.

l. 60. Hephaestus has passed from the hands to the arms, and has secured one of them.

l. 62. 'That he may learn that in clever contrivances he is but a dullard to Zeus.' The participle, where other languages require an infinitive, by a well-known Greek idiom. For σοφιστής cp. l. 944, also l. 459. From the latter passage it will be seen what the σοφίσματα of Prometheus were. In the time of Aeschylus no doubtful reputation attached to the word σοφιστής, which Herodotus (4. 95) applies to Pythagoras, Aeschylus' master, in the sense of a wise, clever man. Observe the incongruity between the adjective and the substantive. 'A more stupid clever man.' This figure of speech is often used by Greek poets, and is known as oxymoron (τὸ ὀξύμωρον).

l. 63. (It is now so completely done that) 'none but the victim could find fault with my work.'

l. 64. γνάθον, because it bites into the flesh. Again metaphorically in l. 368. αὐθάδη, because it goes its own way, heedless of the pain it gives. At this command Hephaestus drives a wedge or spike of steel through the effigy which represents Prometheus.

l. 67. δ' αὖ, not 'a second time,' but of remonstrance, as in l. 743, 'what? dost thou shrink?'

l. 68. ὅπως is sometimes used, as here, with the second person of the future indicative, ὅρα or some such word being understood. 'See that the day does not come when thou shalt cry out for thyself' (and not for another).

l. 71. μασχαλιστῆρας, the straps to go under the armpits, securing the body to the rock.

l. 72. 'I must perforce do this: do not thou give needless orders.' To this protest against Strength's meddling and his harsh tones the demon answers, ' Yes, I will give orders if I please, and shout them at you too.' ἀνάγκη. See l. 16. The word is of frequent occurrence in this Play. Here the compulsion arises from Zeus' commands : further on (l. 515) we find that there is a compulsion to which even he must bow.

l. 73. ἦ μὴν, of strong assertion. See ll. 167 and 907. For ἐπιθωύξω cp. l. 277, also ll. 393 and 1041. πρὸς adverbially, as frequently in Homer, and in later poets, cp. l. 696 and l. 929.

l. 74. Here the superhuman size of the effigy seems to be indicated. Hephaestus must climb down that he may shackle the feet.

l. 75. καὶ δή. See above on l. 54. οὐ μακρῷ πόνῳ answers to βίᾳ, and shows that that word in the command was unnecessary.

l. 76. διατόρους, 'piercing' (active sense). So in l. 181.

l. 77. 'Strike heavy blows, even as the master who sets the task is a heavy one.' γε draws attention to οὐπιτιμητής ; he is harsh and therefore the order must be harshly executed.

l. 78. ' Your tongue is as harsh as your form is ugly.' Probably Strength wore a mask of repulsive features.

l. 79. ' Be as soft yourself (σὺ) as you please, but do not therefore taunt me with my harshness.' Strength exults in the repulsive traits of his own character. See on l. 10.

l. 81. ἀμφίβληστρα, the chains around his legs. This was the last part of the process (l. 74); and it done, Hephaestus proposes that they should leave their victim. Strength consents to go, but not without a last jeer, addressed to Prometheus himself, at his helpless case.

l. 82. ἐνταῦθα νῦν. Both adverbs are emphatic. 'Now then is the time to insult Zeus, there when thou art hanging to the rock !' Observe the present tense of the imperatives : 'go on insulting! go on, giving to men what is the Gods' !' θεῶν γέρα. See l. 7.

l. 83. ἐφημέροισι, creatures of the day, i. e. men. See ll. 253, 546, 945. σοί, 'for thee,' 'in thy cause.'

l. 84. οἷοί τε. See on l. 41. ἀπαντλῆσαι. Nautical metaphor (cp. l. 149), lit. to draw off water from the hold of a ship. 'What part of all thy woes can mortal men draw off for thy relief?'

l. 85. 'The Gods give thee no true name when they call thee Prometheus.' Προμηθεύς = 'forethought,' or, as an adjective, 'provident' (προμηθής). In l. 86 it means 'one to take thought for thee.' This way of moralising on the meaning of proper names (παρονομασία) is common enough in Greek. Thus Polyneices (very quarrelsome) in

S. c. T. 577; Helen (ἐλέναυς, that destroyest ships) in Agam. 680. In Shakspeare we have—
'Old John of Gaunt, and gaunt in being old,'
his own name giving him, as it were, a peg on which to hang his melancholy thought. We should observe that the name Prometheus is on the face of it allegorical, so that it ought, more than a common name, to be true to fact (ὀρθώνυμον).

l. 87. The construction follows the sense, as though it ran αὐτόν σε δεῖ τοῦ προμηθησομένου ὅτῳ τρόπῳ, κ.τ.λ. τέχνης. Strength's parting word is one of contempt. 'Thou thyself (artist that thou art) needest one to help thee to come free out of this arrangement,' i. e. of Hephaestus' art. See Appendix A.

l. 88. See Introduction, p. x.

l. 88. δῖος, in its Homeric sense, 'divine,' often used of the powers of nature, sea, earth, etc.; not, as in l. 622, the possessive adjective of Zeus. ταχύπτεροι πνοαί, the winds which rushed past him on his height.

l. 89. ποταμῶν τε πηγαί, the mountain sources of rivers, which were all around him. ποντίων τε κ.τ.λ., 'and thou, Sea, laughing in thy myriad waves.' Hence Keble's 'The many-twinkling smile of Ocean.' In strong contrast to rock and snow is the distant ripple of the sea.

l. 90. παμμῆτόρ τε γῆ: Earth the universal mother (ἡ τὰ πάντα τίκτεται), and specially the mother of the Titans. See on l. 210.

l. 91. The Sun, the God who sees all that passes on the surface of the globe ('the searching eye of heaven'), and so rightly invoked by the dying, by Cassandra (Agam. 1322), by Ajax (Soph. Aj. 846), forms the climax of Prometheus' appeal.

l. 92. The construction is a common one. The verb ἴδεσθε is followed by an accusative, and then by a relative clause *explaining what* he asked them to look upon in him (*epexegetical*). Cp. l. 475, l. 1093, etc. So often in colloquial French.

l. 92. θεῶν . . . θεός. See on l. 19.

l. 93. αἰκίαισιν. See ll. 178, 600; the verb αἰκίζεσθαι occurs in l. 195, and frequently in the Play.

l. 94. διακναιόμενος. See l. 541. τὸν μυριετῆ. Observe the article. 'The countless years of the time appointed me.' The numeral is indefinite. According to one account Prometheus was to hang for 30,000 years.

l. 95. ἀθλεύσω. Cp. ἇθλος in this metaphorical sense in l. 257, and frequently in the Play.

l. 96. τοιόνδ' refers to what has gone before (see on l. 8), and in fact gives the reason for it. The reason why the bondage is to be so long lies in the nature of the bonds. ταγός, 'ruler,' 'commander;' used three times in Aeschylus' play of the Persae, in each case of Persian captains. νέος, with contempt, cp. l. 35.

l. 97. ἐπ' ἐμοί, against me, i.e. to my hurt. Cp. l. 921, l. 1043, l. 1089, for the use of ἐπί, which is frequent in Homer.

l. 98. See on l. 23.

l. 99. 'I groan for my woe, (asking) how it is to end?' πῆ for ὅπη, as in l. 183.

l. 100. τέρματα. This word, a common Homeric one, occurs frequently in this Play. Cp. l. 184. ἐπιτεῖλαι is said to be used like ἀνατεῖλαι, meaning 'to rise,' 'come into being.'

l. 101. He checks his complaints, and takes a prouder tone. προὔξεπίσταμαι. Each part of the compound is expressive. 'I know all thoroughly beforehand.'

l. 102. ποταίνιον. A predicate. 'No pain which shall come will be new to me.'

l. 103. πεπρωμένην .. ἀνάγκης. See on l. 72, and cp. l. 515. Prometheus could submit willingly to fate, for he knew that it was stronger even than his present tyrant, and would bring his release.

l. 105. The simpler order would be τὸ τῆς ἀνάγκης σθένος ἐστὶν ἀδήριτον.

l. 106. Cp. ll. 197–8. 'I cannot be silent, for my heart is hot within me at the injustice: I cannot break silence, for the story of Zeus' behaviour is a painful one to tell.'

l. 107. οἷόν τε. See on l. 41. γάρ goes closely with θνητοῖς, and, as it were, forms one word with it. Thus the rule of the 'final cretic' is not broken. Cp. l. 821.

l. 108. πορών. A 2 aor. form often used by Homer. It occurs four times in this play in the same sense.

l. 109. ναρθηκοπλήρωτον, 'the fount of fire with which I filled a reed.' The compound should be particularly noticed. According to analogy it should mean 'filled with reeds,' the form being passive. But Aeschylus uses such compounds with much freedom. Perhaps the passive sense is always present, but is sometimes reached circuitously. Thus ναρθηκοπλήρωτον is equivalent to οὗ (τοῦ πυρὸς) ἐπληρώθη ὁ νάρθηξ. Cp. ἀδαμαντοδέτοισι in l. 147, and in Agam. 361 ἄτης παναλώτου, that is, ἄτης ὑφ' ἧς πάντα ἑάλωκεν. θηρῶμαι, present, because the effect abides; 'I am he who stole the fire.' Cp. l. 220.

l. 110. Cp. παντέχνου πυρὸς in l. 7.

l. 111. πόρος, 'a great resource.' See l. 59.

l. 112. Cp. l. 8.

l. 113. 'Chained thus beneath the open sky and nailed.' If πασσαλευτός be genuine (the best MS. has πασσαλευμένος) observe the rare use of the verbal adjective and compare l. 592.

l. 115. As a distant noise, presently discerned to be the faint beat of wings, is heard, and a strange sea smell is wafted to Prometheus, he breaks for an instant into a freer metre, soon returning to the more staid anapaests. ἀφεγγής; not to be taken too closely with ὀδμά. 'What sound, what smell is borne to me, while yet there is nought to be seen?'

l. 116. θεόσυτος agrees with ὀδμή. For the word see l. 596, l. 643. κεκραμένη, 'partly one, partly the other.' The triple alternative may sound unpoetical to us, but the Greeks were familiar with the triple division —Gods, Heroes, Men. Cp. Horace, Odes, 1. 12, 'Quem virum,' etc.

l. 117. ἵκετο. The subject is τίς supplied out of the foregoing question. τερμόνιον, 'at the world's end.' See l. 1.

l. 118. θεωρὸς, with genitive, 'on purpose to witness.' ἢ τί δή. δή marks some impatience, 'or if not for that, then for what?' Cp. Prometheus' reception of Ocean, l. 298, etc.

l. 119. δεσμώτην. The word which gives a title to the Play.

l. 121. δι' ἀπεχθείας ἐλθόντ', with dative. This construction is common both with verbs of rest, as δι' ἡσυχίας εἶναι, δι' ἀπεχθείας εἶναι, and of motion, as διὰ δίκης ἰέναι (Soph. Antig. 742). It arises out of the quasi-adverbial use of such phrases as διὰ σπουδῆς, 'hastily.'

l. 123. This was Prometheus' offence; his too great friendliness to mortals. See ll. 11, 228, and l. 239, etc. λίαν (adverb), 'too great to be safe:' it does not convey any notion of regret.

l. 124. The dim sound becomes the distinct beating of wings, and Prometheus dreads the approach of the hated vulture.

l. 126. 'The air rustles beneath the strokes of light pinions.'

l. 127. Prometheus' resolution does not really quail; but he thinks sadly that whoever be coming, it cannot be a friend.

l. 128. See Introduction, p. x. The first words are reassuring, φοβηθῆς answering to his φοβερόν. 'Fear nothing! we are friends.' πτερύγων θοαῖς ἁμίλλαις, i. e. πτερύξιν ἁμιλλωμέναις. Perhaps each nymph had a separate car. προσέβα, 'approaches,' idiomatic aorist, see on l. 144.

l. 129. πατρῴας. Ocean himself comes on the same errand. See l. 284.

l. 132. The noise of Hephaestus' hammering (l. 56, etc.) had startled them. μυχόν. The inner part of the house, where the women lived, but also used of a cave, as in l. 453.

ll. 133-4. Fear and curiosity had chased away the modesty which kept Greek maidens and wives to the house.

l. 135. σύθην, the augment omitted, as in Homer, where the word is common. Cp. l. 181. ἀπέδιλος, 'without stopping to put on my sandals' (as one ought to do when one leaves the house). ὄχῳ πτερωτῷ. Compare Ocean's car, l. 286.

l. 137. τῆς πολυτέκνου. There were 3000 Oceanides according to Hesiod.

l. 138. τε comes unusually late in the sentence. Here we have the Homeric conception of Ocean as a great river encompassing the earth.

l. 141. For προσπορπατὸς see l. 61.

l. 144. φρουράν. See l. 31.   ὀχήσω, frequent in Homer in the
sense of ' to endure.' Observe the future—Prometheus thinks of the long
years of punishment before him. ' In my terror, a mist rushes before
my eyes, ready to break in tears.'   προσῆξεν, an idiomatic aorist.
By the time the sentence is finished, the action is past, and the verb is
therefore represented by the present in English. Cp. ἠλγύνθην in l. 245,
and l. 128 above.

l. 145. εἰσιδούσᾳ, dative of reference, ' to me as I see.' The genitive
(as though agreeing with ἐμοῦ, supplied out of ἐμοῖσι) would be equally
correct, and there are cases where Aeschylus and Sophocles use the
accusative in similar sentences.

l. 146. 'Withering away against thy rocks.' Cp. πρὸς πέτραις in
l. 4.

l. 147. ἀδαμαντοδέτοισι λύμαις, ' the insult of being bound in chains
of steel.' For the adjective see l. 426, and note on l. 109. The passive
sense may easily be seen here.

l. 149. 'New rulers,' lit. steerers. For the nautical metaphor cp.
οἰακοστρόφος in l. 515, see also l. 84. These metaphors are common in
the dramatists. We may remember that Athenians were a sea-loving
people, and that Aeschylus had himself served at Salamis. With νέοι
cp. l. 35.   νεοχμοῖς, perhaps a lengthened poetical variety of νέοις;
ἀθέτως a shortened poetical variety of ἀθέσμως, i. e. unconstitutionally.

l. 151. 'And what once was mighty he now brings to nought.' The
reference is to the might of Cronus which Zeus had now brought to
nothing. πελώρια well expresses the brute strength of the older lords
of heaven; but compare the epithets in l. 407. With the whole passage
compare Agam. 168, etc. ' He (Uranus) who once was great, abound-
ing in might and in courage, can say no word, for his time is past : and
he (Cronus) who came next is gone, for he has met his better and had
the final fall ; but the man who sounds from a willing heart the hymn
of victory for Zeus shall win wisdom altogether.' The Chorus here, in
their first burst of feeling, use strong and almost rebellious language
about Zeus and his government.

l. 152. An earnest wish—'Oh, that he had hurled me,' etc. Compare
the Homeric phrase, εἰ γὰρ Ζεῦ τε πατέρ, κ.τ.λ. Strictly, this is a pro-
tasis with the apodosis suppressed (by aposiopesis). ' Yes, for if he
had hurled me (it had been well !).' So in Exodus xxxii. 32, 'Yet now if
thou wilt forgive their sin— ; and if not,' etc.

l. 153. ἀπέραντον. Again, in l. 1079, of the net of Ate. Words
denoting absence of limit had a special horror for a Greek mind.

l. 154. Τάρταρον. The prison-house of Cronus and the Titans. See
l. 219, and Hom. Il. 8. 13. Tartarus lies as far beneath Hades, as earth
beneath heaven.

l. 155. πελάσας, having brought me near to chains, i. e. thrown me into chains. The word is used intransitively in l. 712, and l. 807. Homer uses it in both senses.

ll. 156-7. 'That so no god, nor any other, might now be exulting over me.' This is a *final* clause (denoting purpose or object) as shown by the negative μή being used. When the past tenses of the indicative are used in such clauses after ὡς, ὅπως, ἵνα, it is always in cases where the principal sentence is a wish that something now out of the question had happened. Compare l. 749; also Soph. O. T. 1389 and 1392. The force of the imperfect and aorist respectively will be understood by comparing these passages.

l. 158. 'Hung up as a plaything for the breeze.' ἐπίχαρτα, with dative; rejoiced over by my enemies. The verbal is stronger than the simple adjective ἐπιχαρῆ in l. 160. See Agam. 704.

l. 160. 'Who is thus hardhearted, seeing that these things are pleasing to him?' The use of ὅστις is like that in l. 38, etc. This is expressed after the looser manner of Homer. A later writer would say, τίς οὕτω πλησικάρδιος ἐστὶν, ὥστε τάδε ἐπιχαρῆ εἶναι αὐτῷ;

l. 161. ξυνασχαλᾷ. An Homeric form; perhaps lengthened from ἄχος.

l. 163. 'Having set (or disposed) his mind, so that it should not yield.' For the verb cp. l. 529.

l. 165. This is the regular construction of πρὶν after a negative principal sentence in the future tense. So l. 176, etc. For other constructions of πρὶν see l. 825 (with infinitive), and l. 481 (with aorist indicative). The verb is Homeric. παλάμᾳ τινὶ, 'by some device,' since Zeus was too mighty for the empire to be wrested from him by the high hand. The Chorus here unconsciously hint at the danger which was really one day to threaten Zeus. See Prometheus' prophecies in l. 755, etc.

l. 167. ἦ μήν, a strong declaration. 'I swear that the day shall yet come when,' etc. Cp. l. 907, also l. 73.

l. 168. αἰκιζομένου. Here a passive, but deponent in ll. 195, 227, and 256.

l. 169. πρύτανις (πρὸ, πρῶτος), 'the prince of the gods.' So used by Pindar, etc., not by Homer. In some Greek states the word was afterwards applied to the chief priest. In the Athenian constitution it bore the meaning familiar to us.

l. 170. The subject to δεῖξαι is ἐμέ supplied out of ἐμοῦ above. Thus χρείαν ἕξει has a double construction, (1) with ἐμοῦ, (2) with ἐμέ δεῖξαι. The latter *explains* the former, that is, gives the reason why Zeus shall have need of Prometheus. τὸ νέον βούλευμ', Prometheus gives a fuller intimation of what this is in the sequel (see l. 761, etc.); and, before the end of the play, rouses the angry curiosity of Zeus. See l. 947. The βούλευμα is the marriage with Thetis. ὅτου, masculine.

Translate, 'That I should show this new device, by what person he is to be stripped of sceptre and honours.'

l. 171. ἀποσυλᾶται, i.e. μέλλει ἀποσυλᾶσθαι, prophetic present; the course of events is even now leading to that result. Cp. ll. 513, 764, 848. The verb is one which in the active takes an accusative of the person and another of the thing: hence when used in the passive with a personal subject it still takes the accusative of the thing.

l. 172. For the attitude of Prometheus towards Zeus' messages, whether coaxing or threatening, see the last Act of the Play.

l. 175. τόδε, this secret, see l. 170.

l. 176. πρὶν ἄν, see on l. 165.   χαλάσῃ, 'release me.' So with simple genitive in l. 256. Cp. l. 1057.

l. 178. αἰκίας (ῑ). See on l. 93.

l. 179. The Chorus' feeling is of mingled admiration of Prometheus' steadfastness, and fear at the boldness of his speech.   ἐπιχαλᾷς. See on l. 176.

l. 181. διατόρος, 'piercing;' cp. l. 76. See Appendix A.   ἐρέθισε, see l. 1045. Augment omitted, as in l. 135.

l. 182. They hasten to show that their fear is not for themselves; and their conduct at the end of the Play well bears this out.

l. 183. πᾶ for ὅπη, which would follow a participle supplied out of δέδια. 'I fear, wondering where,' etc.; cp. l. 99.

l. 184. 'To run thy bark on shore and see the end of thy voyage.' The verb is used by Aeschylus, (1) transitively, as κέλσαι ναῦν; (2) with an accusative of the land reached; (3) absolutely, i. e. without a noun following. Here it is probably used in the last way, τέρμα being governed by ἐσιδεῖν. For τέρμα cp. l. 100, and for the nautical metaphor l. 149. For the character of a tyrant to whom there is no direct access cp. Soph. O. T. 596-7, where Creon, arguing that it is better to have the practical power than to be the tyrant, says—

νῦν πᾶσι χαίρω, νῦν με πᾶς ἀσπάζεται·
νῦν οἱ σέθεν χρῄζοντες ἐκκαλοῦσί με:

the tyrant not being directly approachable by his subjects.

l. 185. ἀπαράμυθον. Shortened poetical variety for ἀπαραμύθητον. See on l. 150. ᾱ, as in ἀθάνατος always, in ἀπάλαμος, and like words, where metre requires.

l. 186. The irresponsible τύραννος keeps justice to himself; cp. l. 404.

l. 187. ἀλλ' ἔμπας. See on l. 48.

l. 188. μαλακογνώμων, i.e. μαλακὸς τῇ γνώμῃ. Other compounds of γνώμων preserve its proper meaning, as προβατογνώμων, a judge of sheep, etc. For liberties taken by Aeschylus in forming compounds see on l. 109.

l. 189. ταύτῃ, i.e. in the way mentioned above.

l. 190. ἀτέραμνον, the opposite of τέρην, used by Homer as an epithet of κῆρ. See l. 1062.

l. 191. The expression is borrowed from the Homeric hymn to Hermes, l. 524, and well expresses the complete reconciliation which should come about.

l. 192. The zeal for reconciliation shall be *mutual*. See on l. 19.

l. 193. γέγων'. Perfect imperative; this perfect is often found in Homer. The form γεγωνέω occurs frequently in this Play, γεγωνίσκειν is also used.

l. 194. ποίῳ, for ὁποίῳ, cp. l. 182. αἰτιάματι, cp. l. 255.

l. 195. αἰκίζεται. See on l. 93.

l. 197. For the mixed feelings with which Prometheus begins his tale see on l. 106. Here what he says is suggested by the last words of the Chorus, εἴ τι μὴ βλάπτει λόγῳ, with which compare l. 763.

l. 199. The apodosis begins with ἐνταῦθ' ἐγὼ in l. 204. ἐπεὶ τάχιστα means 'as soon as ever,' τάχιστα being joined idiomatically with ἐπεὶ, though logically it should belong to the apodosis, cp. l. 228. εὐθέως is used in the same way. Compare the use of εὐθέως and αὐτίκα with participles; thus αὐτίκα γενόμενος, 'as soon as he was born.'

ll. 201–3. 'Some wishing,' etc. The nominatives are in apposition to words supplied out of the preceding lines, as though the passage had run ἐπεὶ ὡροθύνοντο οἱ δαίμονες στασιάζοντες πρὸς ἀλλήλους, οἱ μὲν, κ.τ.λ. A good parallel is found in Soph. Antig. 259 :—

> λόγοι δ' ἐν ἀλλήλοισιν ἐρρόθουν κακοί,
> φύλαξ ἐλέγχων φύλακα.

A passage which also illustrates the rather loose use of ἀλλήλοισιν here.

l. 202. 'That Zeus might rule, as they were pleased to say.' ἀνάσσοι, optative, because the time of the principal verb is past. δῆθεν, ironice; cp. l. 986. ὡς with ἀνάσσοι is the *final* conjunction, 'in order that:' with ἄρξειεν in the next line it is still the relative adverb 'how,' following σπεύδοντες, and we may thus see how it came to be used in final clauses.

l. 204. 'Giving the best advice to the Titans was unable to persuade them.' βουλευόμενος would be more usual in prose. Cp. l. 1030.

l. 205. Prometheus, though sometimes called a Titan (as in Soph. O. C. 56), was not, according to Aeschylus, a son of Earth, but of — Themis. But see below on l. 210.

l. 206. αἱμύλας δὲ μηχανὰς, 'my politic devices.' So the Titans in their eagerness for armed strife called Prometheus' advice.

l. 208. 'They thought they would be able to conquer without effort, and to rule by the strong hand.' ἀμοχθί, adverb, from ἄμοχθος; cp. ἀνοιμωκτὶ (ῑ), Soph. Aj. 1227, but ἐγερτὶ (ῐ), Soph. Antig. 413.

l. 210. πολλῶν ὀνομάτων μορφὴ μία, 'one form with many names;' possessive or attributive genitive. Here Gaia and Themis are said to be but one person. But in l. 874 Themis is spoken of as Τιτανὶς, and in Eum. 1, Themis is the daughter and successor of Earth. How shall we reconcile this contradiction? Probably the personality of these early nature deities was very vague, and there was a tendency to form one person out of two or more names with which legend associated like attributes. So Earth and Rhea, Rhea and Demeter, etc. In l. 1091 Prometheus seems to address Earth as his mother.

l. 212. In direct contrast to the views of the Titans (l. 208).

l. 213. 'That those who had got the upper-hand must rule by policy.'

l. 216. 'As I was laying all this before them.' The word implies an authoritative exposition, as of one who explains mysteries. Cp. l. 702. 'Much the best of the courses open to me then seemed to be,' etc. The actual best was impossible, for the Titans would not have it: this was δεύτερος πλοῦς. Cp. Agam. 1053, τὰ λῷστα τῶν παρεστώτων λέγει. 'She gives the best advice which your present (bad) case allows.'

l. 218. ἑκόνθ' ἑκόντι. See on l. 19, and l. 192. συμπαραστατεῖν, a military metaphor: to fall in by Zeus' side. Cp. l. 31.

l. 219. 'And so it is due to my advice that Tartarus' deep dark vault now covers the aged Cronus, and all his company.' For Tartarus see on l. 154. μελαμβαθής, an Aeschylean compound.

l. 220. καλύπτει, 'hid, and now hides.' Cp. l. 109.

l. 221. αὐτοῖσι συμμάχοισι. An Homeric idiom. Cp. l. 1047. τοιάδ'. See on l. 8.

l. 223. This is the usual construction of this compound, and of the simple verb ἀμείβεσθαι.

l. 224. The attitude of suspicion which a Greek tyrant had to maintain towards all around him is well illustrated by Oedipus' behaviour to Creon in the Oedipus Tyrannus; cp. l. 184. The general sentiment here expressed would be thoroughly welcome to Aeschylus' audience from their own experience of tyrants at home and from what they knew of them in the Eastern world and elsewhere.

l. 226. The antecedent to δ is τοῦτο. αἰτίαν καθ' ἥντινα κ.τ.λ. explains what that was. δ' οὖν, 'however that may be.' It marks the passage from the general reflection about tyranny to the subject in hand. Cp. Agam. 224. For another use of δ' οὖν see l. 935.

l. 227. αἰκίζεται, see on l. 93, and l. 195.

l. 228. ὅπως τάχιστα, see on l. 199. εἰς here, and elsewhere, follows a verb of rest (to sit), because a previous action (to take my seat) is presupposed. Conversely ἐν after verbs of motion, where rest follows. Both usages are Homeric.

l. 229. νέμει, 'he proceeds to distribute,' present of vivid narrative.

ll. 230, 1. διεστοιχίζετο ἀρχήν, 'set about ordering (i.e. organising) his kingdom.' Cp. ἐστοίχισα, l. 484.

l. 232. The order of the sense is ἔχρῃζεν ἀϊστώσας τὸ πᾶν γένος φιτῦσαι ἄλλο νέον. According to one account given by Hesiod, Zeus did utterly destroy the second (silver) race of men because they did not honour the gods.

l. 234. τοισίδ', 'these plans of Zeus.'

ll. 235, 6. The absence of a connecting particle from the second verb gives boldness to the account. ἐξελυσάμην βροτοὺς τοῦ ... μολεῖν would have been sufficient, the genitive of the fate from which they were saved. μὴ is introduced from another construction implied in the sense and present to the writer's mind, ἐξελυσάμην βροτοὺς ὥστε μὴ κ.τ.λ. Compare the construction in l. 248, and l. 627.

l. 237. τῷ τοι. 'Therefore it is that,' etc., the article for the demonstrative, as in Homer. For τοι see l. 8.

l. 239. 'Setting mortals before myself as objects of pity.' τούτου, sc. οἴκτου. For the thought cp. ll. 83, etc.

l. 241. ἐρρύθμισμαι, 'I am reduced to order,' i. e. 'punished;' thus—Ζηνὶ δυσκλεὴς θέα, 'A spectacle which does little honour to Zeus.' The mind of Zeus' victim has room for shame at the disgrace done to Zeus by his own conduct. See l. 106. and l. 197.

l. 242. Such metaphors are common in Homer. Compare Horace's 'Illi robur et aes triplex circa pectus erat,' etc.

l. 243. ξυνασχαλᾷ. See on l. 161.

l. 244. Here there is a hypothesis implied, as εἰ παρῆν μὴ ἰδεῖν οὐκ ἂν ἔχρῃζον εἰσιδεῖν. See on l. 10.

l. 245. ἠλγύνθην, an idiomatic aorist, where we should use the present. See on l. 145. The Chorus disclaim the idea that it was the mere curiosity of seeing pain which brought them here. See l. 118.

l. 246. καὶ μὴν, used to express assent to what has gone before: 'Well, I allow, that to friends I am a pitiful object.' φίλοις, emphatic. For καὶ μὴν in other senses see l. 459 and l. 1080.

l. 247. The question is put diffidently, 'Did you perhaps go even somewhat further than this?'

l. 248. Literally, 'I stopped men that they should not see death before them.' For the negative see l. 627, and note on l. 236. Observe that the usual construction of παύω would be either παύειν βροτοὺς τοῦ προδέρκεσθαι or παύειν βροτοὺς προδερκομένους, not παύειν βροτοὺς προδέρκεσθαι. Prometheus interfered twice between Zeus and men, (1) by protesting against their wholesale annihilation; (2) by blinding their eyes to the death which Zeus had in store for them hereafter, so that they might not live in slavish awe of him. See Appendix A.

l. 249. τὸ ποῖον. The article is used here (as often) with ποῖον because the φάρμακον was something definite. Not 'quale remedium?' but 'quale hoc remedium?' Cp. Soph. O. T. 120.

l. 250. τυφλὰς, which made them blind to the future. According to another version of the story, it was at the express command of Zeus that Prometheus stopped men from looking forward to death (Plato, Gorgias).

l. 252. πρὸς τοῖσδε, in addition to the greater boons just named. Thus the gift of fire takes a subordinate place. See on l. 7. ὤπασα, cp. l. 30.

l. 253. καὶ, when it begins a question, commonly raises a difficulty. 'Do you really mean to say that men now have fire?'

l. 254. 'Yes; and from it they shall learn many arts.' Cp. παντέχνου πυρὸς in l. 7. The future is used, because Prometheus had only started men on a long series of discoveries. The use of γε in an affirmative answer, showing that something further follows, is well known. See on l. 397.

ll. 255-8. See Appendix B.

l. 256. αἰκίζεται. See on l. 93. κοὐδαμῆ χαλᾷ (σε) κακῶν. 'And in no wise gives thee respite from ills.' See on l. 176. ἄθλου, this word is used several times in the play, of toil, suffering. See on l. 96. προκείμενον, there is an allusion to the phrases ἆθλον πρόκειται, a prize is offered to competitors, and ἄεθλος προκέεται (Hdt.), a contest is instituted.

l. 258. γ', gives emphasis to ἄλλο, and refers it to the latter part of the line. Observe that here Prometheus' release is made to depend upon the mere pleasure of Zeus; in l. 771, etc. it is to be ἄκοντος Διὸς, by the action of Fate which is above Zeus. Here he means any *speedy* release.

l. 259. 'What hope for thee either from the character of Zeus, or from the nature of thy ἁμαρτία?'

l. 260. In full οὔτ' ἐμοὶ καθ' ἡδονήν ἐστι λέγειν. So the infinitive follows adjectives, as in l. 197.

l. 261. The nymphs wish to hear no more of so sad a tale; their woman's wit turns to look for something to be *done*.

l. 263. ''Tis easy for him who has his foot free to advise the unfortunate.' ὅστις, sc. τοῦτον ὃς ἂν κ.τ.λ. The metaphor was a familiar one. Thus 'clearing his foot from the slough of ruin,' of Orestes (Cho. 297), and conversely in Pindar, 'Let the son of Sostratus know that he has his foot in a lucky sandal' (Ol. 6, 11). Aeschylus refers to an old proverb or γνώμη. Prometheus, who is somewhat impatient of advice (see ll. 335, etc.), gently puts that of the Chorus away as beside the mark. He was quite aware of his offence, even when he was committing it, though he had never thought that Zeus would have taken it so seriously.

l. 265. Observe the imperfect, 'I was quite aware while I was doing.'

l. 266. This admission is in answer to l. 260.

l. 267. 'It was by helping men that I found for myself these sufferings. I well know that.'

l. 268. γε emphasises ποιναῖς. 'But as for punishments, I never thought that mine would be so severe.'

.l. 269. Cp. πέτραις προσαναινόμενον in l. 147. πεδαρσίοις, Doric for μεταρσίοις: the form occurs again in l. 710 and l. 916. Cp. αἰθέριον κίνυγμα in l. 158.

l. 270. τυχόντα, 'having for my portion.' Cp. l. 20.

l. 271. καί μοι, 'and now, I pray you,' (ethical dative).

l. 272. He invites them to descend from their cars (see l. 128), and hear out the tale of his coming sufferings, from which they shrink.

l. 274. The request is put very urgently before they consent.

l. 275. τοι (gnomic) shows that Prometheus is upon some old saying, see on l. 39. 'We all know that affliction lights now on one, now on another, but the manner of visitation is one for all' (ταὐτά). This is given as a reason why they should share the trouble of him who for time being is the sufferer (τῷ νῦν μογοῦντι), since their turn may come another day.

l. 276. For the juxtaposition see on l. 29. Here the special force is that of *distribution*, 'to one at one time, to another at another.' But to get the juxtaposition, the natural order of the words (ἄλλοτε πρὸς ἄλλου) is altered; cp. l. 921.

l. 277. 'Not to unwilling ears didst thou utter this cry of woe.' For ἀκούσαις see on l. 23; and for the verb l. 73.

ll. 279, 280. They now descend, and place themselves on the orchestra, in front of Prometheus, ready to hear his story. κραιπνόσυτον θᾶκον. Explained by l. 131.

l. 281. ἁγνὸν, because pure and bright.

l. 282. πελῶ, future, from πελάζω, here used intransitively. See on l. 155.

l. 284. See Introduction, pp. xi, xii. ἥκω, 'I am come;' see on l. 1. δολιχῆς, the home of Ocean lying in the west. The sense is διαμειψάμενος κέλευθον ὥστε πρὸς τῷ τέρματι εἶναι, and the expression is suggested by the frequent use of τέρμα with a genitive in periphrasis. Cp. l. 184.

l. 286. For the winged animal which drew Ocean's car see l. 395. We are told that it was a griffin, and that such grotesque animals were frequently introduced into the Greek theatre.

l. 287. 'By my own will, without a bridle.'

l. 288. Observe how Ocean intrudes his sympathy, and see on l. 18. The words ἴσθι, δοκῶ, are characteristic of his verbose style and pompous character, as are the details in ll. 286, 7.

l. 289. τὸ ξυγγενὲς, cp. l. 39. Ocean was himself a son of Gaia.

l. 291. 'And, over and above relationship, there is none to whom I would wish to pay greater respect than to you.' The phrase μοῖραν νέμειν τινὶ ('morem gerere alicui') is connected with ἐν μοίρᾳ ἔχειν, and, more remotely, with the idea of just distribution of spoil, etc. The construction is like that of the Latin relative with the subjunctive. The optative (without ἂν) is rarely thus used. Compare the construction in ll. 470-1, also that in ll. 904-6.

l. 294. χαριτογλωσσεῖν, to speak for the mere sake of giving pleasure. Ocean protests that it is not in him to do so, he is ready with his deeds. φέρε, cp. l. 544. Used, like the Homeric ἄγε, adverbially before another imperative.

l. 298. ἔα, of surprise. 'Oho! what is all this?' cp. l. 687. καὶ σὺ δή, 'Do you mean to say that you, of all people, are really come?' For καὶ in a question expressing surprise see on l. 253. δή emphasises the pronoun. πόνων .. ἐπόπτης, cp. l. 118.

l. 299. 'How did you dare to leave your ocean-bed?' A sarcasm at Ocean's acquiescence in the rule of Zeus. But he was always a stay-at-home. See Iliad 20. 7.

l. 300. The stream which shares your name. Cp. ῥόος ὠκεάνοιο.

l. 301. 'Caves self-built,' i. e. hollowed out by the sea. σιδηρο-μήτορα .. αἶαν, because iron came to Greece from the north and east of the Euxine: cp. l. 714.

l. 303. ξυνασχαλῶν, pres. 'And because you grieve with me.' For the word cp. l. 161, and l. 243.

l. 304. θέαμα, 'a show-sight.'

l. 305. Cp. ll. 219, etc.

l. 306. For the construction of an accusative explained by a relative clause see on l. 92.

l. 307. γε gives a particular emphasis to the word which it follows : 'I see, Prometheus, and am ready to advise you too, mark that!'

l. 308. ποικίλῳ, 'clever,' 'versatile.' A rather doubtful compliment; cp. l. 206.

l. 309. 'Know thyself,' i. e. learn your true strength and weakness. Even before the phrase γνῶθι σεαυτὸν became current, this would sound like a platitude. Addressed to Prometheus, whose strength lay in his foreknowledge, the words have a very hollow ring. μεθάρμοσαι τρόπους νέους. 'Change your ways, assuming new ones.' This is a case of *prolepsis* (like 'scuta latentia condunt,' etc.). It is well paralleled by Eum. 490, νῦν καταστροφαὶ νέων θεσμίων.

l. 310. See on l. 35.

l. 312. 'Zeus, though he shut himself up (like a τύραννος) far away in his Olympian palace, may hear your words.' At the end of the Play Zeus does hear Prometheus' proud words, and sends Hermes with threats and punishment. See l. 944.

l. 313. ὥστε, κ.τ.λ. The consequences of Zeus' hearing such words. Prometheus' present sufferings shall be but child's play to those which shall follow. See l. 1014. Observe the unusual order of the words for τὸν νῦν παρόντα ὄχλον μόχθων. But there is uncertainty as to the reading.

l. 316. ζήτει, present. 'Set yourself to seek.'

l. 317. 'My advice may sound old-fashioned, but it is to the point.' In the next lines, as in l. 329, Ocean seems to bring in some old-fashioned saws or γνῶμαι.

l. 319. 'Such are the wages of the over-proud tongue.' Cp. Soph. Antig. 126, Ζεὺς γὰρ μεγάλης γλώσσης κόμπους ὑπερεχθαίρει: the reason of the punishment of the Argive chiefs.

l. 320. οὐδέπω. Ocean assumes that it is only a matter of time.

l. 322. 'If you will condescend to take a lesson from me you will not put out your leg against the pricks.' The metaphor, taken from an ox kicking, occurs in Agam. 1624, and in the New Testament.

l. 324. οὐδ᾽ ὑπεύθυνος, i.e. a τύραννος, not responsible like a magistrate in a free state. See on l. 186.

l. 325. 'I will go and try if haply I may be able.' In l. 338 Ocean is more confident of success.

l. 328. ἢ οὐκ form one syllable by synizesis. ἀκριβῶς, ironical. 'Don't you understand to a nicety, for all your cleverness that,' etc.

l. 329. See on l. 317. προστρίβεται, pass. 'is inflicted.' προστρίβεσθαι is more often used as the middle voice.

l. 330. Prometheus answers by a rather dry congratulation.

l. 331. Observe the construction. πάντων μετασχὼν .. ἐμοί would be quite regular, meaning, 'having shared all things with me.' Here καὶ τετολμηκὼς, i.e. καὶ τετολμηκὼς μετ᾽ ἐμοῦ, is inserted between the participle and the dative. Cp. Soph. Antig. 537, καὶ ξυμμετίσχω καὶ φέρω τῆς αἰτίας, and see above on l. 51.

l. 332. μηδέ σοι μελησάτω, sc. ἐμοῦ. The aorist imperative with μὴ is unusual, but more so in the second person. Cp. l. 1002.

l. 333. With the form of this line compare l. 718, and for Zeus' character cp. l. 185.

l. 334. πάπταινε, again in l. 1034. Here it is sarcastic, 'Be very cautious lest you take a mischief yourself on the way.'

l. 335. It has an ironical force. 'Well, I must say you are much better at advising your neighbours,' etc. φρενοῦν, inf. after ἀμείνων, cp. l. 59, and l. 197.

l. 336. ἔργῳ, by what I actually see.

l. 337. 'I must really beg that you will not check one who is anxious to serve you.'

l. 339. ὥστε explains τήνδε δωρέαν. Observe that ἐπαινῶ, like Lat. *benignè*, is sometimes used as a civil formula for declining an offer.

l. 340. τὰ μέν, i. e. in point of zeal.

l. 342. οὐδὲν ὠφελῶν ἐμοί is added to explain μάτην more fully.

l. 343. εἴ τι καὶ πονεῖν θέλεις. 'If your zeal does really extend to action.'

l. 344. 'You are out of the mischief (so ἐκτὸς αἰτίας in l. 330); better keep so.'

l. 345. οὕνεκα, a preposition.

l. 347. οὐ δῆτ', 'Not I.'   κασιγνήτου. Atlas was, according to one account, a son of Iapetus; to another, himself one of the Titans.

l. 348. Atlas is placed by Hesiod in the islands of the West, that is, the Canary islands, his presence there being perhaps suggested by the Peak of Teneriffe. Later mythology places him in Africa. The same poet makes him actually bear up the weight of the heaven. In Homer (Od. 1. 53) he only has the charge of the pillars which keep heaven and earth apart. See Virgil, Aen. 4. 246-251, and Paley's note on this passage l. 350.

l. 350. See Appendix A.

l. 351. Typho, or Typhoeus (the latter is the form used by Hesiod), the last-born of Earth's giant brood; who, after the overthrow of the Titans, threatened Zeus' supremacy, and was smitten by a thunderbolt. He had a hundred heads, from which came voices and sounds of all sorts; and now that he is in Tartarus all the winds which vex seamen come from him. See Horace, Od. 3. 4. 53.   Κιλικίων, because Asia Minor was liable to volcanic disturbances.

l. 354. The rhythm of this line is unsatisfactory. But the reading is uncertain.

l. 355. The rhythm and wording of this line are characteristic of Aeschylus, and suit well the object described.

l. 356. 'And from his eyes was he flashing a dreadful light.' The verb is intransitive, and σέλας is a cognate accusative, as though it were ἤστραπτεν ἀστραπήν.

l. 357. 'Ready, you would think, to wreck Zeus' kingdom.' ὡς with the future participle of the probable effect, as it appears to a bystander.

l. 358. ἄγρυπνον βέλος. According to Hesiod, Typhoeus would have been successful but for the great vigilance of Zeus.

l. 359. καταιβάτης, Ionic form of καταβάτης, 'descending from the sky.' Ζεὺς καταιβάτης is the god who comes down in thunder and lightning (Jupiter Elicius).

l. 360. 'Struck him down from his proud boastings.' Cp. Soph. Ant. 126. The expression here is bold.

l. 361. 'Struck to the very heart.' φρένας, the parts about the heart and breast. The blow was first directed against the hundred heads, and then passed to the vitals.

l. 362. ἐφεψαλώθη, a rare word; φέψαλος occurs several times in Aristophanes.

l. 363. παράορος, Epic παρήορος, 'sprawling.' So Homer, Il. 7. 156, ἔκειτο παρήορυς ἔνθα καὶ ἔνθα. The word is also used of the trace-horse (σειραφόρος or παράσειρος).

l. 364. στενωποῦ, i. e. the Straits of Messina. In l. 351 Aeschylus had spoken as though Typho were imprisoned in Cilicia. Here he agrees with Pindar, who calls Aetna 'the windy press (ἶπον) which holds down Typho.'

l. 366. Here the forge of Hephaestus is placed on the top of Aetna. Virgil (Aen. 8.) places it inside the mountain.

l. 367. Here there is a clear reference to an Eruption of Aetna. See Introduction, p. xviii.

l. 368. γνάθοις, metaphor from the devouring nature of fire. Cp. l. 64.

l. 369. The fertility of Sicily made it of great importance in Roman history. γύας, masc. from γύης.

l. 370. τοιόνδε, gives the reason why Sicily shall be wasted by fire; see on l. 96.

l. 371. 'With the missiles of hot, insatiable, fire-breathing spray.' The reading is uncertain. See Appendix A.

l. 372. 'Mere mass of cinders though he be, he shall yet spout out vapour and flame.'

l. 373. Cp. l. 322. Prometheus will not force his advice upon Ocean, as the latter had done upon him.

l. 374. ὅπως ἐπίστασαι. A sarcasm at Ocean, who well knew how to take care of his own safety.

l. 375. ἀντλήσω, 'will bear to the uttermost.' See on l. 84; and for Prometheus' resolution cp. l. 103.

l. 376. 'Until such time as the temper of Zeus ceases from its wrath.' The genitive, as though with παύεσθαι, cp. l. 634. See also l. 27. ἔς τε has the same constructions as ἕως and πρὶν, except that of the latter conjunction with the infinitive. See l. 458 and l. 697.

l. 377. The sense of the dialogue which follows runs thus:—*Oc.* Do you not know that soft words are sovereign for an angry spirit (such as that of Zeus)? *Pr.* Oh yes, if you approach him at the right moment. *Oc.* What harm then in an attempt, so it be a prudent one? *Pr.* First you lose your trouble, and secondly you show weak compliance. *Oc.* If that be a weakness, I choose it; to be right at heart, yet not to seem to be so, for me! *Pr.* But if you interfere, I shall perhaps get the credit of it. *Oc.* That's a reason for my going straight home. *Pr.* Yes, before you get at cross purposes yourself. *Oc.* With Zeus? *Pr.* Yes! *Oc.* I think I will take warning from you, and go. *Pr.* Pray go! οὔκουν Προμηθεῦ, κ.τ.λ. Cp. Samson Agonistes, ll. 184–6:—

> 'Apt words have power to swage
> The humours of a troubled mind,
> And are as balm to festered wounds.'

l. 378. There is some uncertainty about the precise reading here. Doubtless there is a reference to some γνώμη.

l. 379. Prometheus knew that, in his own case, the convenient time would come, though on a distant day. See l. 167.

l. 380. The metaphor, in this and the last line, is medical, of treating a tumour or the like, and is suggested by ἰατροὶ λόγοι in l. 378.

l. 381. This is a sort of *hendiadys*; that is, the two verbs express one compound action, 'a cautious venture.' Ocean puts the caution first.

l. 383. περισσὸν, 'excessive,' i. e. wasted trouble. So περισσὰ πράσσειν, Soph. Ant. 68.

l. 384. τήνδε . . . νόσον, i. e. εὐηθίαν, or the course of conduct which Prometheus had stigmatised as such.

l. 385. κέρδιστον, 'the most profitable course.' The conduct which Ocean proposes to himself is the same as that suggested in l. 381. He now says that he will put up with being called εὐήθης so long as he is really right at heart. εὖ φρονεῖν is 'to be loyal to one's friends,' 'right-hearted;' φρονεῖν, 'to be sensible.'

l. 387. It is a generous thought for Prometheus' safety which first makes Ocean think of going, but Prometheus at once supports it by the argument that it will be the safer course for Ocean himself.

l. 388. 'Yes, take care lest,' etc. Cp. the construction in l. 68.

l. 389. The construction is continuous with that of the last line, the dative following εἰς ἔχθραν βάλῃ. Observe that in this part of their conversation, which Zeus might have taken amiss, Ocean has been careful not to utter his name. θακοῦντι, used without a case in l. 313.

l. 392. στέλλου, 'start;' lit. 'be packing up.' Prometheus is tired of Ocean's presence, and will not lose this chance of being rid of him.

l. 393. For the construction cp. l. 23 and l. 277.

l. 394. 'My griffin is chafing the smooth air, and I am sure he will be glad to be in his own stable.' For οἶμον cp. l. 2. ψαίρει. The action of a restless horse is suggested, though the verb itself is said to be used of sails flapping.

l. 395. For Ocean's 'griffin' see l. 286. τᾶν, i. e. τοι ἄν.

l. 396. κάμψειεν γόνυ, i. e. in rest. Cp. l. 32. Prometheus is now silent, and the Chorus, ranged around the thymele, begin the first stasimon.

l. 397. 'I groan over thee because of thy fate.' The construction of the genitive is like that which follows οἰκτείρω (as οἰκτείρω σε θεσφάτου μόρου, Agam. 1321), and is perhaps suggested by it. Cp. use of θαυμάζω. οὐλομένας, used here, as in Homer, for an adjective in the sense of ὅλοος.

l. 399. δακρυσίστακτον . . . ῥέος, 'A stream in which tears are made to trickle' (δάκρυα στάζεται). See on l. 109.

l. 401. νοτίοις παγαῖς. By a natural metaphor the eyes are called κλαυμάτων πηγαὶ (Agam. 888). Cp. Soph. Antig. 803. Here the in-

strumental dative is used rather loosely; we should expect some word
meaning 'streams' rather than 'fountains.' ἀμέγαρτα .. τάδε, 'in
this unenviable manner.' Adverbial or cognate accusative after ἐνδεί-
κνυσιν αἰχμάν.

l. 402. ἰδίοις νέμοις κρατύνων, cp. l. 150 and l. 186. The words form
a parenthesis.

l. 405. 'Shows his proud victorious might among the older race of
gods;' (of which the Chorus had just seen an instance in the humiliation
of their father, Ocean.)

l. 406. λέλακε (ᾱ), perfect with present sense. The word is found
with a cognate accusative, as λέλακε στόνον, which is here replaced by
the neuter adjective. So 'dulce loqui,' etc.

l. 407. The adjectives are predicates. 'They (i. e. men, dwellers in
every country) groan for the old glories of thee and thy kindred, so grand,
so time-honoured.'

l. 410. ὅποσοι. The antecedent is θνητοί.

l. 415. 'Their neighbouring home in holy Asia.' ἔποικον is thus
used in Soph. O. C. 506, but more often like μέτοικος for a colonist,
settler.

l. 416. μάχας, genitive after ἄτρεστοι, 'Not to be turned back from
the fray.' The Amazons are meant.

l. 417. Σκύθης ὅμιλος, a multitude, rather than a nation.

l. 419. See l. 2.

l. 420. 'Αραβίας. This word is probably wrong in our text, for
Aeschylus would never have spoken of Arabia as extending to the
Caucasus. In l. 421 θ' is unmetrical. See Appendix C.

l. 424. βρέμων, 'roaring in the battle of keen spears.' Description
of a wild and warlike people.

l. 425. 'The only case I ever heard of like this was that of thy brother
Atlas, whose punishment sea and land bemoan.'

l. 426. See Appendix A.

l. 428. For Atlas see on l. 348. The mention of him there has
suggested his name to the Chorus.

l. 430. See Appendix A.

l. 431. 'As the peoples about Asia condole with Prometheus, so do
sea and land with Atlas.'

l. 433. Ἄϊδος, an Homeric form, used like other forms of the genitive
for the house of Hades. μυχὸς γᾶς, the innermost part of the earth;
i. e. the abyss of Hades which lies beneath sea and land.

l. 435. The ποταμῶν πηγαί were specially called to witness his sufferings by Prometheus, l. 89. ἀγνορύτων, 'pure and liquid.' The
simple ῥυτὸν is a frequent epithet of water in the poets.

l. 436. See Introduction, p. xii.

l. 437. συννοίᾳ, 'deep anxious thought.'

l. 438. προσελούμενον. This is a very rare word, being only found once in Aristophanes (Frogs, 730), and once in a later writer who probably quotes from this passage. The general sense of the word—'insulted, down-trodden'—is quite clear; not so the derivation and form.

l. 439. καίτοι. The incongruity between his services to Zeus and their reward is the subject of his σύννοια. τοῖς νέοις τούτοις. Contemptuous.

l. 440. Because Prometheus was at the right hand of Zeus when the latter was organizing his new kingdom. See l. 230.

l. 441. 'You would know all about this before I should tell you.' For the construction cp. l. 23 and l. 277.

l. 442. The story of the woes of mortals (before I interfered), how I made them, etc. ὡς explains πήματα.

l. 444. ἔννους ἔθηκα, I put in possession of sense, cp. l. 848. ἐπηβόλους (Lat. *compos*), from ἐπιβάλλω; the form is Epic.

l. 445. Not blaming men for their vile state; it was not their fault; the dative as though with μέμφεσθαι.

l. 446. ἐξηγούμενος, cp. l. 214.

l. 447. οἵ, the antecedent is ἀνθρώποις. The relative is used like οἵτινες (see on l. 38) and introduces the reason of the word εὔνοια being used. 'Seeing, saw to no purpose,' like—

'Sheep or goats
That nourish a blind life within the brain.'

l. 448. 'Hearing (with their ears) they did not hearken (with their understandings).' There is no inherent difference between the two verbs.

l. 449. ἀλίγκιοι. Epic word. Homer more often has ἐναλίγκιος. In Agam. 82 the same image is used for extreme old age, which in its feebleness 'wanders like a dream into the daylight.' τὸν μακρὸν χρόνον, the long, unmarked time which they had to live.

l. 450. They mixed up all things (i. e. knew no distinctions of time or place) but lived at random (i. e. on the impulse of the moment). Cp. Soph. O. T. 978, where Jocasta is made to say that εἰκῆ ζῆν, that is, a life without πρόνοια, is best.

l. 451. προσείλους, built to face the sun : opp. to the sunless caves.

l. 454. They could not distinguish the seasons of the year.

l. 456. βέβαιον. Applies to all the seasons. 'No sign, at least none on which they could depend.'

l. 457. ἔς τε, with past tense of indicative. See on l. 376. δὴ emphasises, 'until such time as I,' etc.

l. 458. There was a special difficulty in observing the *settings* of stars.

l. 459. καὶ μὴν, used here, as often in the orations, when a new and important argument or topic is ushered in. Cp. l. 1080, also l. 247.

Number underlies most arts and sciences, hence its primary importance. Remember that Aeschylus was a Pythagorean, and therefore likely to extol arithmetic. For σοφισμάτων see on l. 62.

l. 460. γραμμάτων τε συνθέσεις. Methods of joining letters (to form syllables and words).

l. 461. Mythologically the Muses were the daughters of Mnemosyne, and practically Memory is the power which produces all poetry and letters (ἁπάντων ἐργάτιν). That men were originally without this gift seems to follow from Prometheus' account (ll. 447, etc.), though in what sense he gave it to them he does not tell us.

l. 462. κνώδαλα, wild fierce animals, such as oxen and horses before they were tamed. The word is used several times by Aeschylus.

l. 464. 'That with their bodies they might relieve mortals in their heaviest toils.' For διάδοχοι see l. 1027. Literally 'successors in toils.' Horses are thus considered the partners and helpers of men; they 'love the rein' too; and thus stand above the κνώδαλα, which drudge and 'are slaves to their harness,' and by which the poet chiefly means oxen.

l. 466. Horses were much kept for racing, and their possession was a mark of luxury. Cp. the use of ἱπποτρόφος in Demosthenes, de Corona. For the praises of the horse see Soph. O. C. 708.

l. 467. 'It was I and none else,' lit. 'none else instead of me.' So in Soph. Ajax, 444, οὐκ ἄν τις αὔτ' ἔμαρψεν ἄλλος ἀντ' ἐμοῦ.

l. 468. ναυτίλων ὀχήματα, i. e. 'ships.' The mention of this and of the last discovery recals the language of Sophocles in the second Chorus of the Antigone (l. 332, etc.), where the power of man, shown in his different conquests over nature, is set forth.

l. 470. σόφισμα. Cp. l. 459.

l. 471. ἀπαλλαγῶ. The subjunctive after the relative is unusual, and the construction seems to resemble the Latin ('non habeo artificium quo liberer'). Cp. l. 291, where the optative without ἄν, and l. 906, where the optative with ἄν, are so used. Here the subjunctive almost represents the future ἀπαλλαγήσομαι: in Homer the future indicative and aorist subjunctive are often used alike. See on l. 561. See also Goodwin's Moods and Tenses, § 71. For the general thought cp. l. 86 and l. 239.

l. 472. αἰκές, i. e. ἀεικές. Cp. l. 93. The words of the Chorus are suggested by those with which Prometheus ended. He whose strength had been his forethought and self-reliance, and who had guided bewildered men, now seemed to give himself up, like a quack physician whose confidence fails him when he is himself ill.

l. 474. 'And canst not find by what drugs thou shouldest thyself be treated.' For the construction see on l. 92. ἰάσιμος, sc. εἶ.

l. 476. The metaphorical physician of the Chorus suggests to Prometheus a fresh item in the list of his benefits to men.

l. 477. This line explains τὰ λοιπά. For πόρους cp. l. 59 and l. 111.

l. 478. εἴ τις ἐς νόσον πέσοι, 'as often as any one fell ill.'

l. 479. ἀλέξημ', 'a specific.' The terms which follow refer to the different modes of applying medicines; solid drugs, ointments, draughts: medical details are frequently found in Aeschylus. See on l. 380.

l. 481. πρίν γ', 'until such time as.' γε emphasises πρίν. So ἔς τε δὴ with aorist indicative in l. 457.

l. 483. We are again reminded of Soph. Ant. 361-2.

l. 484. 'I arranged the different methods of the divining art.' With the verb cp. διεστοιχίζετο in l. 230.

l. 485. 'Which dreams were to be held waking-visions.' The two terms are often contrasted. Thus in Homer οὐκ ὄναρ ἀλλ' ὕπαρ. Of the importance attached to dreams, and the care given to their interpretation we have abundant proof in Aeschylus. See line 645, etc.

l. 486. κληδόνας, any sounds of ominous import; 'bos elocuta,' and the like.

l. 487. συμβόλους (συμβάλλω), sc. οἰωνοὺς, 'Signs which met them on their journeys.' Cp. Agam. 104, also Horace, Od. 3. 27. 1-7.

l. 488. γαμψωνύχων, as vultures or eagles. σκεθρῶς, cp. l. 102.

l. 489. 'Both which were propitious in their kind, and which sinister.' These were in fact the signs which appeared to the right and left (of an observer turned to the north) respectively, the former direction suggesting the brightness of the East, the latter the gloom which follows sunset.

l. 490. εὐώνυμος ('of happy name') is an euphemism, i. e. an auspicious word used to express what was really inauspicious. So Eumenides ('kindly ones') for Erinnyes ('wrathful ones'). A knowledge of the habits of different classes of birds was part of the diviner's art.

l. 492. στέργηθρα, 'loves.' The word properly means 'love tokens.' ξυνεδρίαι, 'the numbers and modes in which they would congregate.'

l. 493. 'The plumpness and the most acceptable colour.' τίνα for ἥντινα, cp. l. 99. With the passage generally cp. Soph. Ant. 1009.

l. 496. Perhaps there is an allusion to the childish story of Prometheus' fraud upon Zeus in distributing the flesh of an ox, which forms part of the legend in Hesiod, but is ignored by Aeschylus. See Introduction, p. vii.

l. 498. φλογωπὰ σήματα, i. e. τὰ τῶν ἐμπύρων.

l. 499. ἐπάργεμα, properly said of eyes darkened by cataract. See on l. 479.

l. 500. 'So much for these things.' He now passes to minerals.

l. 503. ἐξευρεῖν. The subject is ἑαυτὸν, but the Greek language allows this to be attracted into the same case as the subject to φήσειεν, and thus, like the nominative of all personal pronouns, when not emphatic, omitted; cp. line 561.

l. 504. 'Unless he wished to make an idle vaunt.'

l. 505. συλλήβδην, 'in a single sentence,' as given in the next line.

l. 507. The enclitic νυν attached to imperatives, or, as often in Homer, to imperative adverbs, as εἶά νυν, δεῦρό νυν, preserves no sense of time. Here it is used in a coaxing argument, 'do not now,' etc. Cp. l. 997, and observe the short quantity in both cases. καιροῦ πέρα. Cp. πέρα δίκης in l. 30. ὠφέλει, present imperative, 'be a helper of mortals.' This is a case where the real prohibition is contained in the *second* (δέ) clause of the antithesis, the first (μέν) being in sense only subordinate. 'Do not, *while* you are careful to help men, neglect yourself!' This is common in prose, and is characteristic of the Greek language.

l. 509. This hope of the Chorus rested on nothing but their wishes, and their sense of Prometheus' greatness. Aeschylus is fond of touching on the credulity of woman, and her eagerness to hope what she wishes. ἔτι, not temporal, 'yet,' i. e. 'in spite of present appearances.'

l. 511. ταύτῃ, 'in the way you mean.' Prometheus smiles at the idea of a solution suggested by the Chorus. Time and Fate are his only deliverers. Μοῖρα, see on l. 516. πω. The Chorus were wrong not only as to the manner of the deliverance, but also in thinking it would come presently.

l. 512. πέπρωται. A passive perfect from πόρω, whose 2 aor. we have in l. 108. This tense is usually impersonal, as in l. 519, but we have ἡ πεπρωμένη μοῖρα, from which the construction in the text easily follows.

l. 513. ὧδε, 'then and only then,' i.e. after long years of torture. So οὕτω δή after participles, etc., in Attic Prose. φυγγάνω, 'I am to escape.' See on l. 171.

l. 514. τέχνη, the art of Hephaestus which had bound him there. Cp. l. 87. ἀνάγκη. That inner and impersonal condition of things by which they are what they are. Cp. l. 16. See Horace, Od. 1. 35. 17, where Necessity is personified as the attendant of Fortune.

l. 515. οἰακοστρόφος, the 'controller,' lit. steerer. Cp. l. 149.

l. 516. The Fates, the three beings who spin the threads of human destiny, are by Aeschylus identified, or closely connected, with the Erinnyes. As the name Μοῖραι imports, they distribute or assign to each, whether god or man, his proper place, and see that it is kept. Thus in a certain sense they are superior even to the gods. In the Eumenides, Aeschylus has described a conflict of power between these great primeval deities and some of the gods of Olympus, ending in a thorough and final reconciliation. μνήμονες. The Erinnyes watch the shortcomings of men, and never forget nor forgive.

l. 517. The Chorus shrink from the apparent inference that there is a power yet stronger than Zeus. See their next question, l. 519.

l. 518. γε shows a limited assent, 'Yes, in the sense at least that he cannot,' etc. Cp. l. 768.

F

l. 520. 'You have now (οὐκέτι) come to a question which I cannot answer for you.'

l. 521. ἦ που, 'Is it perhaps?' a diffident question. σεμνὸν, 'solemn,' 'mysterious.' Forbidden to ask directly, the Chorus try to peep round the corners of the secret.

l. 522. μέμνησθε. Homeric. 'Bethink ye of some other subject.' In the next Act Prometheus becomes more communicative.

l. 523. συγκαλυπτέος, suggested by ξυναμπέχεις above.

l. 525. ἐκφυγγάνω. 'I am to escape.' Cp. l. 513.

l. 526. Second stasimon. See Introduction, p. xiii. 'May Zeus never set his might against my will!' i.e. may I never so act as to come to cross purposes with Zeus.

l. 527. For θεῖτο cp. l. 163.

l. 529. 'Nor may I be idle in approaching the gods at their holy feasts, by the ever-flowing channel of my father Ocean.' It was the duty of the Ocean nymphs to grace with their presence and songs the table of their father when the gods came to visit him in his home. So Iphigeneia graced the table of Agamemnon (Agam. 242). Where παρά is used with the accusative, there is commonly some idea of 'motion towards;' which may here be supplied out of ποτινισσομένα.

l. 530. 'Nor may I ever offend in my words!' The third article in this simple outline of the 'whole duty' of a sea-nymph.

l. 536. Here we have the affirmative side of the picture, the prayer that an innocent and happy life may be hers. 'Sweet methinks it is (so) to link day to day by bright hopes (that even the long life of an immortal (τὸν μακρὸν .. βίον) may not seem too long).'

l. 539. ἀλδαίνουσαν. Epic word, found several times in Aeschylus.

l. 540. This innocent dream of life suggests by contrast the awful reality of Prometheus' position.

l. 541. μυρίοις μόχθοις, suggested by his words in l. 512. δια-κναιόμενον, cp. l. 94. A word of four syllables appears to be wanting here. There is no break in the sense.

l. 543. αὐτόνῳ γνώμᾳ. 'Self-willed spirit.' Thus the Chorus attri-bute to Prometheus the same fault which he found in Zeus. (The word αὐτόνῳ, though not found in any MS., fairly gives the sense of the passage.) σέβει θνατοὺς, a forcible expression, since 'worship paid to mortals' sounds at first almost a contradiction in terms.

l. 545. φέρ' ὅπως, i.e. φέρε ἰδὲ ὅπως κ.τ.λ. See on l. 294. 'See, see for thyself, friend, how bootless this boon: say, where is any help found for thee?' ἄχαρις χάρις. 'A favour (to men) which brings little thanks (to thee).' Not, as the words might mean, 'a favour which is no favour.'

l. 546. ἐφαμερίων, possessive genitive. 'What help have creatures of a day (cp. l. 83) to give?'

l. 547. ἄκικυν. Homeric word.

l. 548. ἰσόνειρον (ῑ), suggested, as are the other expressions about man's helplessness, by the words of Prometheus above. See l. 448.

l. 550. ἐμπεποδισμένον, sc. ἐστί. 'Never shall the devices of mortal men transgress the appointed order of Zeus.' In these words, though spoken here in character, and expressing the inability of men to help or hinder in the contest between Zeus and Prometheus, we may read Aeschylus' own wording of a truth which is the keynote of this, as of his other plays. See Introduction, p. xviii.

l. 553. τάδε. the truths just uttered.

l. 555. 'That strain which now rises to my lips is the very opposite to that which I raised when I sang thy marriage hymn,' etc. This would be, more simply expressed, τὸ μέλος ὃ ἀρτίως μοι προσέπτα τὸ διαμφίδιον ἦν ἐκείνου ὃ ᾖδον ὅτε ὑμεναίουν κ. τ. λ. τὸ διαμφίδιον suggests the idea of a pair of opposite things (hence the article, as in τοὐναντίον, there being only one opposite to any given thing); but instead of the other member of the pair being given in the genitive (ἐκείνου), both members of it are enumerated (τόδ' ἐκεῖνό θ'). For two things connected by τε or καὶ or both, when in sense they are to be taken disjunctively, cp. l. 927. προσέπτα, idiomatic aorist; see on l. 144. For the verb cp. l. 115.

l. 556. λουτρά, part of the marriage solemnity.

l. 557. ὑμεναίουν, 'when I was singing the wedding song;' in which nymphs, as attendants of the bride, joined.

l. 559. ἰότατι γάμων, i.e. ἕνεκα γάμων. The word is often used in Homer in such phrases as θεῶν ἰότητι, 'by the will of the gods.' ἕκητι, which alone is used in similar phrases in the Odyssey, is by later poets used as a preposition, by Pindar in both senses, the old and the new. We may suppose that Aeschylus here uses ἰότητι in a similar fashion, though it may still preserve some of its original meaning, 'in zeal, good will for thy marriage.' The word is not so used elsewhere. τὰν ὁμοπάτριον, 'our sister,' literally, our own father's daughter. ἕδνοις, here used of gifts given by the suitor to the bride. An Epic word. The dative is instrumental, but not to be taken closely with πιθών.

l. 561. See Introduction, p. xiii.

l. 561. φῶ, 'am I to say?' deliberative subjunctive. This is another case in which the aorist subjunctive is shown to resemble in use the future indicative. See on l. 471. τίνα φῶ λεύσσειν (sc ἐμέ). Cp. l. 503.

l. 562. χαλίνοις.. πετρίνοισι. 'Bonds (not of leather but) of rock.' The substantive is metaphorical, the adjective literal. See on l. 880.

l. 563. χειμαζόμενον. Cp. l. 15, δυσχειμέρῳ.

l. 564. 'What offence can have deserved such a punishment?'

l. 567. χρίει, 'stings.' See l. 598. The word means properly, 'to rub,' hence also 'to anoint.' τις, 'somehow, I know not how.' In her frenzy she mixes up with this gadfly the phantom of Argus the herd, killed by Hermes but still seeming to haunt her.

l. 568. ἄλευε δᾶ. She calls on any one who will hear to keep the dreadful phantom off. Cp. l. 687.   δᾶ is usually taken to be a Doric form for γᾶ. See Appendix A.

l. 570. δόλιον ὄμμα, which sees all ways at once. Cp. μυριωπὸν above.

l. 572. περῶν, more often transitive, as in l. 792.

l. 573. ἀνὰ τὰν παραλίαν ψάμμον. As about the shore of the Adriatic. See l. 836.

l. 574. Here Io's song becomes antistrophic, the four lines spoken by Prometheus below dividing strophe and antistrophe.   ὑπὸ, i.e. in response, echo to my complaint. The preposition belongs to ὀτοβεῖ, being separated from it by tmesis. Cp. ὑπηχεῖν, etc.   κηρόπλαστος, the reed fastened by wax, i.e. the panpipes played by the herdsman Argus, and still sounding in Io's ears.

l. 575. ὑπνοδόταν νόμον. Cognate accusative after ὀτοβεῖ, 'a drowsy strain, (which yet does not let me sleep).'

l. 576. She dwells passionately on the word 'wanderings.' Cp. l. 585.

l. 579. Like Prometheus (l. 268), she acknowledges that she had erred, but complains that the punishment is cruelly disproportionate.

l. 582. Cp. l. 747, also l. 152.   ποντίοις δάκεσι, 'the monsters of the deep.' Cp. Horace's 'scatentem beluis pontum.'

l. 583. Observe the construction of φθονήσῃς here, and cp. l. 626.

l. 585. See on l. 576.

l. 586. γεγυμνάκασιν. Lat. 'exercuerunt.'

l. 587. ''Tis I, the horned maiden, who speak.'   κλύεις, idiomatically, at the end of a speech, as in l. 683..

l. 589. Prometheus takes up the word κλύεις.   'Hear? that I do, and 'tis the voice of Inachus' daughter.' The epithet shows that he is acquainted with her story.

l. 590. θάλπει, present, because the description still applied to Io, 'the kindler of Zeus' heart.' See on l. 109.

l. 591. δρόμους. Cognate accusative after γυμνάζεται, as though it were τρέχει δρόμους.

l. 592. Ἥρᾳ στυγητὸς, 'hated by Hera.' A participle would be more natural, στυγηθεῖσα. The use of the verbal adjective as one of two terminations is very rare. Nor is στυγητὸς found elsewhere in Classical Greek, except in compounds, as θεοστύγητος (Choeph. 635). For γυμνάζεται cp. l. 586.

l. 593. Io, astonished at Prometheus' address, which shows that he knows her name and story, asks who he is and what he can tell her as to her future.   πόθεν, i.e. πόθεν μαθών.

l. 594. ἄρα, inferential. She wonders who he is because he called her by her right name.

l. 595. The construction is double accusative after προσθροείς, ἐτή-τυμα being in sense equivalent to an adverb. Cp. l. 401.

l. 596. θεόσυτον, cp. l. 116.

l. 597. ὠνόμασας, i.e. in the word οἰστροδινήτου, l. 589. χρίουσα, see on l. 567. φοιταλέοις, in active sense, 'maddening.'

l. 600. Her disgrace and grief lay in the wild, beast-like movements with which she was compelled to hurry over the earth without food or sleep. Cp. l. 674. νήστισιν, applied to the wanderings which kept her fasting.

l. 601. λαβρόσυτος, cp. κραιπνόσυτος, l. 279.

l. 602. 'The poor and wretched can at least rest and eat. but Io cannot.'

l. 605. τέκμηρον. The active voice is rare, the middle alone being found in Homer.

l. 606. τί for ὅτι, as in l. 493.

l. 607. εἴπερ οἶσθα. She is inclined to believe him because he knew her name, also because in her misery she would catch at any straw. See on l. 509. Afterwards (l. 824) Prometheus is careful to give her *proof* of his prophetic power.

l. 609. He gives a full and free consent to her request; and, in answer to her first question, begins by telling her who he is. τορῶς, as she had asked him to do (l. 604).

l. 610. Not after the fashion of oracles. ἁπλῷ λόγῳ, see l. 46.

l. 611. 'It is due to friends to show no reserve.' Prometheus and Io were fellow-sufferers, and therefore friends.

l. 613. κοινόν, i. e. to the whole race of men.

l. 614. τοῦ δίκην, 'in punishment for what?' Cognate accusative after πάσχεις, rather than in apposition with τάδε. The use of χάριν as a preposition arises from a similar construction.

l. 615. ἁρμοῖ, 'lately,' like ἀρτίως in sense. The word is used by Theocritus. Prometheus' pride recoils from telling his woes to every comer.

l. 616. 'Will you not then give this boon to me?' A gentle request, as, in l. 52, οὔκουν with the future indicative is a strong command. For the verb cp. l. 108.

l. 617. 'You might (if you wished) hear anything from me.'

l. 618. φάραγγι, cp. l. 15. ὤχμασε, cp. l. 5.

l. 619. Δῖον, possessive adjective of Ζεύς. See on l. 88.

l. 621. τοσοῦτον. 'So much as I have already said.' ἀρκέω is found used in two different ways, ἀρκέω σαφηνίσαι, i.e. 'valeo enuntiare,' and ἀρκέω σοι, i.e. 'sufficio tibi.' Here perhaps some of the second meaning is present as well as the first. 'I can say no more, and you must be content.'

l. 622. 'Then at any rate (if you will not tell me more about yourself) tell me also, besides what you have already said, the limit of my wandering, what time shall be (i.e. bring) it.' The construction is complete at δεῖξον; what follows is added to show in what sense she used τέρμα, i.e. of a limit of *time*.

l. 624. Aeschylus often dwells on the thought that it is happier for men not to know too much about the future. Cp. l. 248, and Agam. 251; so Horace—'Prudens futuri temporis exitum | Caliginosa nocte premit Deus.' But cp. l. 101 for Prometheus' feeling about this in his own case.

l. 625. Double accusative after κρύψῃς. 'Celare' in Latin has the same construction.

l. 626. 'I do not grudge thee this boon,' explained by l. 628. For the construction, which is found in Homer with this verb, cp. l. 583.

l. 627. Here the infinitive takes the negative because of the negation implied in μέλλεις, and the double negative μὴ οὐ because of the pre-ceding negation implied in the question τί μέλλεις; See lines 787 and 918, also Soph. Ajax, 540, and O. T. 13. For γεγωνίσκειν cp. l. 193.

l. 628. θρᾶξαι (perhaps rather θράξαι), varied form of ταράξαι.

l. 629. 'Do not be more delicate about my feelings than is agreeable to me.' ὡς apparently for ἢ ὡς. There are passages in Attic Greek which perhaps bear out this use of ὡς. It is well to remember that the particles and adverbs which express comparison are originally very simple ones, ἤ, τε, etc. Here the Latin would be 'magis *quam* quod mihi dulce est,' i e. 'by the standard of what is pleasant to me,' which may be the meaning of ὡς here. See also on l. 555.

l. 631. 'Please not yet!' The future of Io's wanderings will be of little interest to the Chorus, who do not know her past story.

l. 634. τὰ λοιπὰ δ᾽ ἄθλων. 'What remains in the way of toils;' cp. l. 684. In prose it must be τὰ λοιπὰ (or τὸ λοιπὸν) τῶν ἄθλων.

l. 635. 'It rests with you, Io, to serve them and do them a favour.' χάριν, cognate accusative after the neuter verb. Cp. l. 614. So Herodotus has χρηστὰ ᾿Αθηναίοισι ὑπουργέειν.

l. 636. 'More particularly seeing that they are your father's sisters.' Inachus was a son of Ocean.

l. 637. The infinitives are in the aorist, 'To weep and have done.'

l. 638. 'In a quarter where one is sure to win the meed of a tear.' As Io would do in telling her tale to her kinswomen. For the optative μέλλοι see Goodwin's Moods and Tenses, § 63, 4 (*b*).

l. 639. 'Is spending time to good purpose.' τριβὴ χρόνου or βίου is the rubbing away, passing, of life. Cp. Soph. Ant. 1079, οὐ μακροῦ χρόνου τριβή.

l. 640. Observe the absence of caesura. See Introduction, p xx. ἀπιστῆσαι, 'to distrust,' as though they might make a bad use of the knowledge.

l. 641. σαφεῖ ... μύθῳ. As frankly as Prometheus had promised to speak on his part, l. 609.

l. 642. 'I am ashamed even to tell of,' etc. For the construction see on l. 92. The special disgrace was the quarter from which the trouble came, ὅθεν.

l. 643. θεόσσυτον, see l. 596, and observe the form here. χειμῶνα, 'storm of woes.' Cp. l. 1015.

l. 644. προσέπτατο. Appropriate to the metaphorical word χειμῶνα, rather than to διαφθοράν, which stands nearest.

l. 645. πολούμεναι, Lat. 'versatae,' but with idea of motion. The Homeric form of the verb is πωλέομαι, participle πωλεύμενος.

l. 646. παρθενῶνας. The rooms in the house occupied by the un-married daughters. So ἀνδρῶν κ.τ.λ.

l. 648. δαρέν. Cp. l. 940. ἐξόν, neuter absolute, σοι being closely attached to ἐξόν, and forming, as it were, one word with it; the rule of the 'final cretic' is not broken. Cp. l. 107.

l. 649. ἱμέρου βέλει, 'the shaft of love,' a frequent metaphor. Cp. Agam. 744.

l. 650. For τέθαλπται cp. l. 590. πρός, 'by,' lit. 'from thee:' cp. l. 92. So used in Homer. ξυναίρεσθαι Κύπριν, 'to join in acts of love.' The verb sometimes takes a genitive.

l. 653. The natural order is πρὸς τὰς ποίμνας καὶ τὰς βουστάσεις τοῦ πατρὸς (Ἰνάχου).

l. 654. 'That so, if so it may be, the eye of Zeus may rest from its desire.' See on l. 10, and for λωφήσῃ πόθου cp. l. 376.

l. 656. ξυνειχόμην, 'I was constrained.' Often used of physical con-straint, as with πόνῳ, δίψῃ, κ.τ.λ. ἔς τε δή, 'till the time came when.' See on l. 457.

l. 658. 'To Pytho, and off for Dodona.' The latter oracle being more distant, the more vague preposition ('in the direction of') is used. ἐπί is so used by the historians.

l. 659. θεοπρόπους. Like θεωρούς. 'Messengers sent to inquire of a god.' Literally, 'those who declare what the gods reveal' (πρέπω). ἴαλλεν, imperfect, 'he sent relays of messengers.' ὡς μάθοι, 'in order that he might learn.' Optative as following a past verb. τί χρή, for ὅτι χρείη. We have already (as in l. 493) had τί for ὅτι, the direct for the indirect interrogative pronoun; here a like change takes place as to the part of the verb used.

l. 660. δρῶντ᾽ ἢ λέγοντα. The participles contain the real verbal notion : 'What he must do or say in order to please the Gods.' δρᾶν, 'to do a deed.' πράσσειν, 'to act,' or 'to transact.'

l. 661. αἰολοστόμους. 'Shifty, riddling.' So the Theban Sphinx is called ἡ ποικιλῳδός.

l. 663. τέλος, adverbially used, 'at last.' ἐναργὴς βάξις, opposed to the χρησμοὶ ἄσημοι above.

l. 664. 'Clearly charging him in so many words.' The two parti-

ciples contain one idea : hence the infinitive ὠθεῖν, governed in syntax by
the former of them, in sense by both.

l. 666. ἄφετον, agreeing with ἐμὲ, and to be taken with ἀλᾶσθαι,
'sent free to wander (like some sacred animal) over earth's remotest
bounds.' ὅροις, used vaguely, like Latin *finibus*, or our 'bounds.'

l. 667. 'And (threatening) that if he did not do so a bolt should
come.' If the participle understood were ἀπειλοῦσα, or the like, we
should expect ἂν μολεῖν.

l. 668. ἐξαϊστώσοι, future optative, because in the oratio recta the
future indicative would be used.   This mood is rare.

l. 671. ἄκουσαν ἄκων. 'He loth as I.' See on l. 19. 'Spite of
his unwillingness, he must needs comply, for the bit of Zeus was in
his mouth.' Cp. Agam. 217, 'When he put on the collar of necessity,'
also said of a father sacrificing his daughter to obey a prophet's message.

l. 672. πρὸς βίαν, 'perforce.' Cp. l. 208.

l. 674. She was represented on the stage with horns like a cow.
Cp. l. 588.

l. 675. 'Stung by the sharp bite of the gadfly.' For χρισθεῖσ' see
on l. 597.

l. 676. ᾖσσον, imperfect. The change was so sudden that she
found herself all at once rushing with maddened plunge.   Κερχνείας
ῥέος, uncertain.

l. 677. Lerna was a small lake, giving its name to part of the coast
of Argolis. Argus is called a son of Earth. Cp. l. 567.

l. 678. ἄκρατος ὀργὴν, 'of temper violent.' The words go with
ὡμάρτει. Observe again the imperfect tense.

l. 679. 'Looking with his myriad eyes (see l. 569) at my footsteps,
wherever I went.' κατὰ as in κατ' ἴχνος.

l. 680. ἀφνίδιος, from ἄφνω (ᾰ). The usual form is αἰφνίδιος. Argus
was killed by Hermes.

l. 681. When he was dead, the other tormentor, the gadfly, was sent
by Hera.

l. 682. 'I am driven from land to land.' The phrase occurs in
Aristophanes (Ach. 235) and is quoted by Cicero as if proverbial.
Connect it with such expressions as ἄγειν τινα πρὸ δόμων, 'to lead one
forth in front of the house.'

l. 683. Addressed to Prometheus, although Io's narrative was really
being given for the benefit of the Chorus, since he knew both her past
and her future.

l. 684. λοιπὸν πόνων. 'What remains in the way of toils.' See on
l. 634.

l. 685. 'Do not in thy pity (lit. "having felt pity for me ") cheer me
up with tales which are not true.' Cp. l. 629. νόσημα, metaphorically, as in l. 225.

l. 686: συνθέτους λόγους, ' words made up,' i. e. with intent to please.

l. 687. ἄπεχε, ' keep her (Io) away ! ' cp. l. 568. The maidenly simplicity of the Chorus is shocked by Io's tale, and especially, perhaps, by the calmness of her tone in asking to be told the whole stern truth.

l. 689. ' I used to think in my pride that such words would never never come to my hearing.' The negatives belong in sense to the infinitives: though if they did so in construction they would be μήποτε. Cp. the familiar οὐ φημί, and Eum. 561, where the same verb is used as here.

l. 692. λύματα strictly means ' filth,' ' pollution,' here used for λῦμαι (see l. 148).

l. 693. ψήξειν, ' should rub, wear (as acid wears steel).'

l. 694. For Μοῖρα see l. 516.

l. 696. γε gives an ironical emphasis to πρό, cp. l. 335. ' Well, you do groan in good time.' πρό, adverbial, as sometimes in Homer. This is its original use. See on l. 73. ' And art *as* one full of fear.' This seems to be the force of τις, which is often placed after substantives and adjectives in comparisons ; cp. l. 473.

l. 697. ἔς τ' ἄν. Cp. l. 376. προσμάθῃς, ' Learn in addition to what you have now heard.'

l. 698. τοι has a ' gnomic ' force. See on l. 39. ' It is pleasant, they say, to the sick.' The truth of the γνώμη has been illustrated by the wish of both sufferers, Prometheus and Io, to know the worst. For προὐξεπίστασθαι cp. l. 101.

l. 700. γε in its usual sense of ' at least.' ἐμοῦ πάρα, because it was at his request that Io had told her story. See l. 635.

l. 701. τῆσδε, genitive after μαθεῖν, on the analogy of πυνθάνομαι. Cp. Soph. O. T. 575.

l. 702. This would be at full length, ἐξηγουμένης ἀμφ' ἑαυτῆς τὸν ἑαυτῆς ἆθλον. Thus the words ἀμφ' ἑαυτῆς do double duty, (1) as an epithet of ἆθλον, (2) in the sentence at large. This happens even in prose with other prepositions, as ἀπό, ἐκ. Cp. Agam. 538, Soph. El. 137. For ἆθλον see l. 257.

l. 703. τὰ λοιπά, explained by οἷα χρὴ κ.τ.λ.

l. 704. πρὸς Ἥρας, cp. l. 601.

l. 705. Here he turns to Io, and addresses her alone. The reader will find it hard to follow in a map the wanderings of Io. In that part of them described in this speech (ll. 700–741) she is brought from Scythia, where she was now standing, to Asia, which she enters for the first time at l. 730, by crossing the Cimmerian Bosphorus. To reach this, she is first to go eastwards, avoiding the nomad Scythians and the Chalybes, but keeping along the north shore of the Black Sea, until she comes to a certain river, which is not named, but is said to bear a name descriptive of its furious course. This she is to follow to its source in the Caucasus. By this river is thought to be meant the Hypanis (Kuban), which comes down a white, muddy torrent from the glaciers of the Caucasus. 'Saxosum .. sonans Hypanis.' But (1) this falls into the Cimmerian Bosphorus on its eastern or Asiatic shore, which Io does not reach till long after she has crossed this river; (2) there is nothing in the name Hypanis suggestive of such a torrent. Probably Aeschylus, who only knew the rivers falling into the Black Sea from the accounts of sailors who had never followed them inland, confused the Hypanis with the Borysthenes, taking the mouth of the latter, and the source and general character of the other. As to the name, that of Borysthenes would be sufficiently descriptive; perhaps however the name intended is Araxes (ἀράσσω), a name which is applied to several rivers, and which may have been given by him to the imaginary one above described. Following then the Hypanis to its source in the Caucasus she is to cross the range at that point. There is a pass (the Nakhar) from the head-waters of the Kuban to those of the Kodor and the rich land of Abkhasia, which crosses the chain near (twenty-five miles west of) Elbruz, its highest peak, and, though lofty (9500 feet), is traversed by oxen, and was, until lately, in regular use. As Elbruz is a conspicuous object from the Black Sea, rumours of such a pass might well have reached Greece. (See Grove's Frosty Caucasus, ch. xii.) She is however to cross the range from north to south, and so to reach the Amazons, who will conduct her to the Cimmerian Bosphorus, and so she will have reached Asia. If this is what Aeschylus meant, it follows that he was quite ignorant of the true position of the Caucasus, and must have thought that both it and the old home of the Amazons on its southern side lay north of the sea of Azov and the Don, which he held to be the boundary of Europe and Asia. But see Appendix C.

l. 706. θυμῷ βάλ', 'store up in thy mind,' more commonly ἐν θυμῷ or εἰς θυμὸν, βάλε. ὡς ἂν, 'that so, if haply so thou mayest, thou mayest learn,' etc., see on l. 10. τέρματα, cp. l. 623.

l. 708. Io's general course had been from west to east, but she may have come northwards from the sea to the place where she now stood. Hence the direction to turn her face towards the east. ἀνηρότους, because occupied by nomad tribes. στείχειν does not commonly take any but a cognate accusative, as στείχειν ὁδόν.

l. 709. For ἀφίξει with accusative cp. l. 724.

l. 710. πεδάρσιοι, cp. l. 269. The Scythians are said to live ' in mid air ' because their wattled huts are set upon wheels. Cp. Hor. Od. 3. 24. 19 : 'Campestres melius Scythae, | Quorum plaustra vagas rite trahunt domos.'

l. 712. οἷς μὴ πελάζειν. Infinitive in sense of imperative. For the verb cp. l. 807, and see on l. 155.

l. 713. 'Keeping close with thy feet to the sea-sounding beach (of the Euxine).' The verb is best known in the passive, being used alone, or with a dative. The active voice is here used in the same sense, with a 'cognate accusative' of the instrument of motion. Cp. βαίνειν πόδα; see also Soph. El. 721.

l. 714. 'On the left hand.' The genitive is used in such phrases with or without ἐκ.

l. 715. The Chalybes, workers in iron, really lived south of the Black Sea. Scythia being an iron-producing country (cp. l. 301), the poet has placed them there. See on l. 705.

l. 717. See on l. 705. For ἥξεις with an accusative cp. l. 709, also l. 808.

l. 718. With the form of this line cp. l. 333.

ll. 719, 20. πρὶν ἄν. See on l. 164. ὁρῶν ὕψιστον. So Herodotus says that 'the Caucasus is of all mountains both the greatest in extent and the loftiest.' Both in the height of particular peaks, and in the unbroken elevation of the range, the Caucasus surpasses the 'Alps' of central Europe, though it is far surpassed by the Himalayas. Neither of these however were known to Aeschylus.

l. 721. 'Peaks, neighbours to the stars,' is a bold and thoroughly Aeschylean expression. The epithet is probably suggested by ἀστυγείτονας.

l. 722. 'To the road leading to the south.'

ll. 724–7. αἳ Θεμίσκυραν ... μητρυιὰ νεῶν. This is a parenthesis. These Amazons, whom Io is to find south of the Caucasus (see on l. 705), shall one day settle on the southern coast of the Black Sea. The country of the Amazons was commonly placed somewhat further east, in Colchis.

l. 726. Salmydessus was on the same sea, but on the European side of the (Thracian) Bosphorus, and thus far west of the Thermodon. The name was given to the coast between the promontory of Thynias and the Bosphorus; and from the dangerous character of it and its inhabitants the whole sea got the name of Πόντος ἄξενος, afterwards changed, by euphemism (see on l. 490), to Εὔξεινος (hospitable). γνάθος, because it devours ships (cp. l. 64 and l. 368).

l. 727. 'Step-mother of ships,' because of the unmotherly reception which it gives them (cp. ' Injusta noverca,' etc.).

l. 729. For the accusative after ἥξεις cp. l. 709, etc. ἰσθμὸν, i. e. the Isthmus leading to the Crimea. πύλαις, the Straits, i. e. the Cimmerian Bosphorus. λίμνης, the Sea of Azof, 'which the ancients, considering its shallowness, and the fact that its water is almost quite fresh, more appropriately called a marsh.' (Bryce, Transcaucasia and Ararat.)

l. 731. αὐλῶνα. The Straits above-mentioned, across which Io is to swim.

l. 733. Βόσπορος. 'The ford of the Cow-maiden.' But observe that in all other compounds of βοῦς the diphthong is preserved. ἐπώνυμος. See on l. 85.

l. 734. κεκλήσεται, the future of the perfect, the sense of which it retains. 'Shall have been called,' i.e. 'shall be called for ever.' Cp. l. 840.

l. 735. Cp. l. 709. ἆρα. Here he appeals to the Chorus: 'Do ye or do ye not now think that the tyrant of the Gods is violent in all ways alike (i.e. in the case of Io as of myself)?' It is clear that Io has now for the first time been brought into Asia, and that her passage thither is a climax in her cruel treatment. See Appendix A.

l. 739. Here he turns to Io again: 'A cruel suitor for thy hand in marriage.' μνηστήρ sometimes takes a genitive of the person, as σοῦ.

l. 740. 'As to the tale which thou hast now heard, believe that it has not yet even reached the preface.'

l. 743. δ' αὖ. 'What? dost thou cry and groan?' See l. 67. τί που. 'I wonder what thou wilt do when,' etc.

l. 745. The Chorus, horrified at what they have heard, ask if anything worse can possibly be in store for Io. The reply is chilling. λοιπὸν ... πημάτων. Cp. l. 684.

l. 746. γε, of assent, cp. l. 518 and below l. 768. 'Yes, a very wintry sea of woe and ruin.' The metaphor is a natural one, and is common in Aeschylus and Sophocles. Cp. Soph. O. C. 1240, Antig. 586.

l. 747. ἀλλ' οὐκ, i.e. ἀλλὰ τί οὐκ. 'Why did I not hurl myself (a second ago when I began to speak)?' See on l. 129.

l. 750. ὅπως ἀπηλλάγην. 'That I might have been set free.' The past tense of the indicative is used with ὅπως because the main wish is one the realisation of which would have been in past time. See on l. 156. With this wish of Io's compare that of Prometheus at l. 152. Observe that she could not kill herself because she lacked resolution, he because he was an immortal (l. 753).

l. 753. ὅτῳ. 'Seeing that to me,' see on l. 38 and cp. l. 759. For πεπρωμένον see on l. 518.

l. 754. 'For that would be (at this time of speaking) a release from my woes.'

l. 755. δὲ answers to μὲν in l. 753; but the sentence begins afresh after the parenthesis (l. 754). τέρμα ... προκείμενον. Cp. l. 257.

l. 756. πρὶν ἄν. See on l. 165.

l. 757. ἔστιν. 'Is it possible?' etc. Io is astonished at what seems to be implied in Prometheus' last words. With the whole of this dialogue compare that beginning at l. 507.

l. 758. **οἶμαι.** 'I think (from the way you say that).' **συμφοράν,** the event, issue, i. e. the fall of Zeus.

l. 759. **πῶς δ' οὐκ ἂν** (sc. ἡδοίμην); **ἥτις,** see on l. 753. **ἐκ Διὸς,** 'At the hand of Zeus.' Cp. l. 221, and the use of *πρὸς* in l. 704.

l. 760. The sense is **ἐπεὶ ἔστι τάδε, πάρεστί σοι μαθεῖν ὅτι ἐστὶ (τάδε).** With this use of *ὡς* cp. the phrase *ὡς ὧδ' ἐχόντων.*

l. 761. **τύραννα** for *τυραννικά.* So *τύραννα δρᾶν* in Soph. O. T. 588. For the construction see on l. 171.

l. 762. As the danger was to be averted (see Introduction) from Zeus, this answer to Io's direct question scarcely conveys the truth. We may observe that Prometheus, in speaking of this intended marriage with Thetis and the danger to arise from it, does not himself use the future tense, but the present, which, while it conveys prophetic intimation, does so with some mystery and reserve. See on l. 171.

l. 763. **εἰ μή τις βλάβη.** Cp. l. 197.

l. 764. The verbs are prophetic presents (see above on l. 762), but as their forms in the future are the same, there is an ambiguity.

l. 765. In this question Io touches the very point. It was the marriage with a mortal which was to endanger Zeus.

l. 768. **γε,** of limited assent: 'Yes, in the sense that she shall bear.' Cp. l. 746.

l. 769. This and the lines which follow should be carefully observed, since they contain the key to the future solution of the plot. (See Introduction, p. xvi.)

l. 770. **ἂν** is not to be taken closely with **λυθεὶς** ('if I were released'), but with the sentence generally: 'There is no way of averting the danger, except in the possibility of my being released.' Thus **ἂν** points to an implied condition, **εἰ λυθείην ἐγὼ, ἀποστροφὴ ἂν εἴη.** See on l. 10. But see Appendix A.

l. 772. **χρεών** (sc. **ἐστὶ**); the first item of information as to the deliverer.

l. 773. Io is staggered to find how this news connects her fate with that of Prometheus.

l. 774. For **γε** cp. l. 768. 'Yes, thy descendant in the thirteenth generation,'—literally, 'the third in descent, in addition to ten other generations.' There is no natural difference in sense between **γέννα** and **γονὴ** (cp. l. 853). The line is somewhat oracularly expressed, and so it strikes Io.

l. 775. **οὐκέτ'.** It had seemed clear until these last details were added. **εὐξύμβλητος,** 'easy to guess,' equivalent to **εὐξύμβολος.**

l. 776. Cp. l. 624.

l. 777. **εἶτα** is not strictly temporal; if it were, the participle must have been *προτείνας.* 'Do not, while you proffer me a boon, yet defraud me of it.'

l. 778. θατέρῳ. 'One or other of two boons.' The article is used because, if one of two things is rejected, the other becomes definite. See on l. 555.

l. 779. δίδου, present imperative, 'Offer.'

l. 780. 'Choose whether,' etc. ἤ for εἴτε, as often in Homer. πόνων τὰ λοιπά, see on l. 634.

l. 782. τούτων, 'of these boons.' τῇδε, i. e. to Io.

l. 783. 'Do not deprive me of the compliment of a story,' lit. 'do not dishonour me in the matter of a story.' Cp. Soph. Antig. 22, where the same verb is used.

l. 784. γέγωνε. Cp. l. 193.

l. 785. The Chorus are much more interested in hearing of Prometheus' deliverer than of the future of his fellow-sufferer, although of their own sex.

l. 786. Addressed to Io and the Chorus.

l. 787. For the construction see on l. 627.

l. 789. 'Enter it on the careful tablets of thy mind.' The same metaphor occurs in Eum. 275.

l. 790. 'When thou shalt have crossed the stream which bounds continents.' The narrative is resumed from l. 735, so that the stream in question is the Cimmerian Bosphorus. In the remainder of this speech Io's wanderings are concluded, and she is brought to rest at Canopus on the Delta of the Nile. The intermediate points of the journey are very obscure. Apparently she is taken first to the west of Libya (where the fabulous Cisthene and the Gorgons were), perhaps by a northerly and westerly route through central Europe to Spain, and then across the Straits of Gibraltar. From the west of Africa she would then go across the north of that Continent till she struck the Nile. We cannot doubt that we have lost some, perhaps a large, part of this account.

l. 792. πόντου περῶσα φλοῖσβον, 'passing along the shore of the sounding sea:' i.e. the west coast of Africa, which we must suppose that she has now reached. ἔς τ' ἄν. Cp. l. 697.

ll. 793, 4. 'The plains of Cisthene where the Gorgons dwell.' Little is known about Cisthene, which is said to have been in Libya, at the end of the world. The Gorgons were daughters of Phorcys, and are described by Hesiod as γραῖαι—hence δηναιαὶ κόραι.

l. 795. 'Possessing one eye amongst them.'

l. 796. The far West was spoken of as the region of darkness, because of the gloom which follows the sunset (ποτὶ ζόφον ἠερόεντα).

l. 800. ἕξει πνοάς, i. e. 'shall live.'

l. 801. φρούριον, 'a garrison.'

l. 802. Here he goes back to two terrors which Io must avoid, the griffins and the Arimaspi.

l. 803. γὰρ introduces the description of the δυσχερὴς θεωρία. 'What I mean is, be on your guard against,' etc.   Observe the epithets 'sharp-beaked, unbarking hounds of Zeus;' i. e. creatures with the *ferocity* of dogs, but which have beaks like birds and do not bark, and therefore are not real dogs. See on l. 880; for the griffin see on l. 395.

l. 805.   The Arimaspi are placed by Herodotus in the north of Europe. If therefore the river which flows with gold mentioned in the next line be, as has been thought, the Guadalquiver, Aeschylus is again confusing distant regions.

l. 807.   For πέλαζε cp. l. 712.   The journey is now continued from the coast of Libya.

l. 808.   οἷ, the antecedent (κατὰ σύνεσιν) is φῦλον. 'The fountains of the sun' perhaps only means 'the place where the sun rises.'

l. 809.   This river is thought to have been the Niger, which must then be placed so far from its true position as to make it a boundary of Ethiopia.

l. 810.   'Follow its banks *up* (and then cross the intervening country) until you come,' etc.

l. 811. καταβασμὸν, the fall of the Nile.   There seems to be a confusion between the κατάδουποι, or Cataracts of the Nile, and the καταβαθμὸς or 'steep slope which separates Egypt from Libya.'   Βυβλίνων, an imaginary name, formed from βύβλος, the papyrus-plant.

l. 813. οὗτος, i. e. the Nile ; τρίγωνον, i. e. the Delta.

l. 814. οὗ δή, 'where at last.'   τὴν μακρὰν ἀποικίαν, 'thy distant colony,' i. e. distant from Argos: μακρὸς is occasionally so used.   The Colony is Canopus.

l. 815. πέπρωται, see on l. 519.

l. 816. ψελλὸν, 'inarticulate,' i. e. obscure.   Prometheus wishes to be plain (cp. l. 609), and is ready to be cross-questioned.

l. 817.   'Do not fear trespassing on my leisure, for I have more than I could wish of that.'   The humour and the courtesy of Prometheus are well shown in this line.

l. 819. The Chorus are still impatient (cp. l. 785) to hear about Prometheus and his deliverer.   τι, 'any detail in her wanderings.' παρειμένον, 'passed over by you.'

l. 820. γεγωνεῖν.   See on l. 523, etc.

l. 821. See on l. 107.

l. 822.   'I think you remember what it was.'

l. 823.   More fully ἀκήκοε πᾶσαν τὴν ἑαυτοῦ πορείαν μέχρι τοῦ τέρματος. See on l. 284.   He has finished the story of her wanderings, but there is more to come ; the restoration of Io to her senses, the fortunes of her descendants, and lastly, the birth of that descendant who is to deliver him.   Thus the two stories flow together, and Io and the Chorus are both gratified (see l. 844). But before he reaches this the climax of his prophecy, he turns to Io, and tells her an incident of her *past* wanderings, this proof of his knowledge being intended to dispose her mind to believe what was yet to come.   ὅπως ἄν, see on l. 10, and for the construction of the participle, on l. 62.

l. 825. For other constructions of πρίν see on l. 165.

l. 826. We should rather expect the present participle διδούς, but the idea in his mind is that *when he has given* the proof he shall be believed.

l. 827. 'I will omit the bulk of what I might say, and will proceed to the very end of (that part of) your wanderings, (i. e. from Argos to Dodona).'

l. 830. 'Dodona on its lofty ridge surrounded by the Molossian plains.'

l. 831. 'An incredible wonder, the speaking oaks.' The oracle was given from these oaks by the mouth of two doves.   Soph. Trach. 171.

l. 833. See l. 663.

l. 835. This line is possibly an interpolation; if retained, it should be construed '(the wife) that was to be; does aught of this steal back into your memory?'

l. 836. οἰστρήσασα, 'having become possessed by the gadfly.'

l. 837. κέλευθον, cognate accusative after ᾖξας. The 'great gulf of Rhea' is the Adriatic.

l. 838. 'From whence thou art to be tossed (see on l. 171) by wandering backwards and forwards,' i. e. along the coast of the Adriatic.

l. 840. See on l. 733.   The first syllable of Ἰόνιος is long, and the fourth foot is therefore an anapaest, which is admissible, being part of a proper name.

l. 842. τάδε, his knowledge of the incident just described.

l. 843. 'That it (my mind) sees somewhat more than meets the eye.' He really means that it sees a great deal more.

l. 844. See above on l. 824.

l. 845. 'Having taken up the scent of my old story.' Two constructions are blended, (1) εἰς ταὐτὸν ἐλθὼν τοῖς πάλαι λόγοις. (2) ἐλθὼν εἰς τὸ ἴχνος τῶν πάλαι λόγων.

l. 846. The city Canopus is thus supposed to exist before the colony is founded there by Io's children.

l. 847. 'At the very mouth of Nile, on the alluvial ground there.'

l. 848. ἐνταῦθα δή, 'there at last.' Cp. l. 814.   τίθησιν ἔμφρονα, cp. l. 444.   The tense is again the present of prophecy.

l. 849. 'Stroking thee with hand which shall not scare, and by a mere touch.'   The aorist participle expresses the instantaneous nature of the touch.

l. 850. 'Taking his name from the creative touch of Zeus' (Epaphus from ἐπαφῶν). But see Appendix A.

l. 852. πλατύρρους, cp. εὔποτον ῥέος in l. 812.

l. 853. The fifty daughters of Danaus, who was great grandson of Epaphus. For γέννα cp. l. 774.

l. 856. The cousins were the fifty sons of Aegyptus. The flight of the daughters of Danaus, and their reception at Argos, are the subjects of Aeschylus' play 'The Suppliants.'

l. 856. οἱ δέ, Epic for οὗτοι δέ. ἐπτοημένοι, 'in a quiver,' the epithet is appropriate to the simile of the hawks which follows.

l. 857. λελειμμένοι, with genitive, 'left behind by,' i. e. the pursued had not a long start.

l. 859. The meaning of this line is doubted. It is best taken, 'the god shall grudge them the persons (of the maidens).'

l. 860. δέξεται, sc. αὐτάς.

l. 861. δαμέντων (i. e. τῶν ἀνεψιῶν). For this suppression of the substantive in the genitive absolute cp. Soph. Antig. 910. νυκτιφρουρήτῳ, see on l. 109. Ἄρει, instrumental dative after δαμέντων. Aeschylus passes rapidly over this horrible deed.

l. 862. αἰῶνος στερεῖ. The deed is stated in the barest possible words.

l. 863. σφαγαῖσι, 'the throat.'

l. 864. With this dreadful wish cp. Virgil's milder 'Di meliora piis atque errorem hostibus illum !'

l. 865. This was Hypermnestra. Cp. Horace, Od. 3. 21. 30-end.

l. 867. θάτερον, '*the* one (rejecting the other).' See on l. 778.

l. 868. κλύειν ἄναλκις, 'to be called a coward.' So with adverbs, κλύειν εὖ, 'to be well spoken of,' etc. Compare Horace, Sat. 2. 6. 20, 'Matutine pater seu Jane libentius audis.'

l. 869. And so shall be the ancestress of Alcmena and Hercules. Cp. l. 772.

l. 870. Here, and in l. 876, the infinitive is '*epexegetical*,' i. e. added to explain ταῦτα, and show in what sense 'these things' require a long time. ὥστε with the infinitive would be more usual. Cp. l. 5.

l. 871. γε μήν, 'however, to come to the point.' Cp. the use of δ' οὖν in l. 226 after a digression.

l. 872. I. e. Hercules.

l. 874. For the mother of Prometheus see on l. 210.

l. 875. See above on l. 870.

l. 877. Io, in the interest of listening, has forgotten her torments ; now a fresh paroxysm begins.

l. 877. ἐλελεῦ, a wild cry, here of pain. σφάκελος, 'a convulsion,' cp. l. 1046. ὑπό belongs to ὑποθάλπουσι.

l. 880. 'The arrow point not forged with fire,' i. e. not a real arrow

G

point, but the sting of the fly. This is a good instance of a striking kind of metaphor, of which a slightly different example was noticed on l. 803; to the metaphorical word is attached an epithet, showing, by the absence of some well-known property, that the use is only metaphorical. So in Soph. O. T. a plague is called 'an Ares without brazen shield,' and in the Book of Wisdom the Egyptians are said to have been 'shut up in a prison without iron bars (i. e. of darkness).' For χρίει see on l. 597.

l. 881. 'In my fear my heart kicks against its walls' (lit. the midriff). So Macbeth, 'And make my seated heart knock at my ribs.' The Greeks were accustomed to this physiological way of describing the passions. Cp. Agam. 995.

l. 882. τροχοδινεῖται, a word probably coined by Aeschylus. Cp. στροφοδινοῦνται, Agam. 51.

l. 883. ἔξω.. δρόμου, 'out of a straight course.' The phrase is used more than once by Aeschylus metaphorically; here it has also a literal application to Io's wild course.

l. 884. γλώσσης ἀκρατής, 'losing power over my tongue,' explained by next line.

l. 885. The metaphor is of a turbid river meeting the strong waters of the sea. Woe is the sea (see on l. 746); the other part of the metaphor is bold and unusual. εἰκῆ, because she was γλώσσης ἀκρατής. Cp. l. 450.

l. 887. Io now leaves the stage; and the Chorus in a short ode, which should be compared with the last (ll. 526-560), draws the moral from her ill-matched union with Zeus and its consequences.

l. 887. 'A wise, a wise man was he, who first did weigh this in his mind, and give it utterance with his tongue, that to marry in one's own degree is far best.'

l. 890. καθ' ἑαυτόν, 'according to one's own standard.' We have had covert references to popular sayings or γνῶμαι, as in l. 39 and l. 309. Here we have an express quotation. This saying, 'wed in your own rank,' is found also in other forms.

l. 891. Here follows an amplification of the original γνώμη. 'Neither the rich nor the highborn should be sought in marriage, when one lives on the labour of one's hands.'

l. 893. ὄντα χερνήταν, in apposition to τινα, the subject to ἐραστεῦσαι. γάμων is sometimes, as here, found with a genitive of the person. Cp. τῶν σῶν γάμων in l. 739.

l. 895. Μοῖραι, see on l. 516. λεχέων Διὸς εὐνάτειραν, 'the consort of the bed of Zeus.' πέλουσαν, i. e. οὖσαν.

l. 896. πλαθείην, 'may I approach (in marriage).' For πελάζω see on l. 155. τινὶ τῶν ἐξ οὐρανοῦ, 'any (other) of the gods in heaven.'

l. 898. The reason for the prayer just finished is the sad spectacle of Io. ἀστεργάνορα, 'without wedded love.'

l. 900. 'By the sad, wild, painful wanderings which Hera sent thee.' ἀλατείαις πόνων would be, more simply, ἀλατειῶν πόνοις. Here the antistrophe ends: the remainder of the Chorus perhaps forms another strophe and antistrophe.

l. 901. μὲν corresponds to μηδὲ in the next line. ἐμοὶ, belonging strictly to the first clause, comes somewhat out of place, being put first for prominence. 'For myself, because my marriage is (will be) with my equals, I have no present fear ; and I pray that the eye of none of the greater gods may look upon me (as that of Zeus has upon Io).' The nymphs of the Chorus were living as unmarried daughters in their father's house (l. 130); when they speak of their marriage, therefore, it must be in the future.

l. 904. 'This (resistance to a god-lover) is a war which none should wage.' γε emphasises ὅδε. There are two points to be noticed in ἄπορα πόρ·μος: (1) πόριμος, the verbal adjective of πορεῖν (see on l. 108) used, like a participle, with an accusative case ; (2) there is an apparent incongruity in sense between the two words; you expect πόρους πορίζουσα, and you have ἄπορα πορίζουσα. Compare the figure of speech noticed on l. 62, and translate, ' Rich in the wealth of despair.'

l. 905. 'I know not what would become of me' (were such a love to overtake me). With this and the next line compare the less regular constructions in l. 291 and l. 470.

l. 907. Prometheus breaks into exultation at the thought of the deliverance which he has prophesied, and defies Zeus and his vaunted thunderbolt. ἦ μήν. See on l. 167, and compare that passage generally.

l. 908. τοῖον. See on l. 96, and cp. l. 920. (Οἷον, the reading which has most authority, would mean ὅτι τοῖον).

l. 909. ὅς, i. e. the issue of the marriage, relative κατὰ σύνεσιν, as in l. 808. For this marriage cp. l. 764.

l. 910. See Introduction, p. v.

l. 912. ἥν, cognate accusative after ἤρᾶτο. The antecedent is ἀρά. For δηναιῶν cp. l. 794.

l. 913. Cp. l. 769.

l. 915. χῷ τρόπῳ, sc. δεῖ γενέσθαι αὐτά. πρὸς ταῦτα, 'therefore,' 'in the face of that.'

l. 916. The language is scornful in the extreme, especially the epithets. πεδάρσιοι, cp. l. 269.

l. 918. οὐδέν, 'in no wise.' τὸ μὴ οὐ πεσεῖν, 'so as not to fall.' Really an accusative of result (cognate acc.) after ἐπαρκέσει. For the double negative see on l. 627.

l. 919. πτώματα, a cognate accusative in the strict sense of the term, as is γάμον in l. 909.

l. 920. νῦν. By his present perverseness Zeus is sowing the seeds of future trouble, and preparing the way for this foolish marriage.

l. 921. ἐπ' αὐτὸς αὐτῷ. For the inversion of the order of words see on l. 276, and for ἐπὶ on l. 97.

l. 922. ὃς δή, 'He it shall be who,' etc. As this child never came to the birth (see Introduction, p. xvi), the prophecy here is somewhat too confident. See on l. 762.

l. 924. Prometheus heaps contempt on the insignia of the Olympian sea-god, as above on the thunder of Zeus. Compare the Homeric ἐννοσίγαιος, ἐνοσίχθων. For νόσος see on l. 685.

l. 927. The sense is 'how far apart is ruling *from* serving.' But the Greek words are joined by *copulative* instead of *disjunctive* particles. See on l. 555, and cp. Soph. O. C. 808.

l. 928. The Chorus try to calm his angry mood. This is the conventional function of the Chorus,

　　　　'Regat iratos et amet pacare tumentes,'
but in this case it is thoroughly in keeping with the personal character of the Ocean nymphs.　θήν, used much like δή, but almost exclusively an Epic word.　ἃ χρῄζεις, i.e. 'your wish is father to your evil prophecies.'

l. 929. τελεῖται, things which are in process of being accomplished. πρὸς, adverbial, 'moreover.' Cp. l. 73.

l. 930. 'But is one really to expect,' see on l. 253.

l. 931. καὶ τῶνδε, 'even than what I now offer.' γε emphasises τῶνδε.

l. 933. ᾧ in the sense of ᾧτινι (see on l. 38). 'Seeing that to me,' etc. For μόρσιμον see on l. 516.

l. 935. 'Well then let him do it.' For this use of δ' οὖν, *in defiance*, cp. Soph. Ajax, 961. For another use of δ' οὖν see above l. 226.

l. 936. 'The Goddess from whom there is no escape' (ἀ, διδράσκω), i.e. Nemesis. Either from this passage, or from some earlier saying to which Aeschylus here refers, προσκυνεῖν Ἀδράστειαν, 'to deprecate Nemesis' for what one does or says, passed into common speech.

l. 937. Sarcastic. 'Go on flattering him who for the hour is lord!' in full, ἀεὶ θῶπτε τὸν ἀεὶ κρατοῦντα. For the present imperative cp. l. 82. Prometheus is led by his anger into a reply to the timid suggestion of the Chorus which is less courteous than his general language to them, and will be seen in the sequel to be undeserved.

l. 938. ἢ μηδὲν, we should expect οὐδὲν, but μηδὲν (usually τὸ μηδὲν) is often used where there is an idea of a really existing 'nothing,' here 'a snap of the fingers.'

l. 939. The imperatives are sarcastic. 'This his short time.' Yet the time covered thirteen generations of mortal men.

l. 940. δαρὸν, cp. l. 648. ἄρξει θεοῖς, cp. l. 49.

l. 941. Here he is aware of the approach of Hermes. τρόχιν, the 'runner,' 'lackey.'

l. 943. πάντως, 'assuredly,' cp. l. 16. These new gods are always innovating and harassing. Hermes must have come to announce some new change.

l. 944. Hermes appears as the minister and trusted messenger of Zeus; whose character he reflects, though his language has some of the eloquence and dignity usually attributed to the messenger God. As he has heard Prometheus' last words, the severity of his address is not uncalled for. σοφιστήν. See on l. 62.

l. 945. 'Who sinned against the gods by giving honour to mortal men.' Cp. l. 108.

l. 946. λέγω, 'I mean,' i. e. 'my message is to thee.'

l. 948. πρὸς ὧν, the antecedent is some *persons* supplied κατὰ σύνεσιν out of γάμους. For πρὸς cp. l. 92, l. 761, or l. 767. With γάμων the preposition would naturally be διά.

l. 950. αὔθ' ἕκαστ', 'the very details of it all.'

l. 952. τοῖς τοιούτοις, 'by such words, threats, as yours.'

l. 953. γε, ironical, as in l. 335. 'Yes, the speech is well rolled out, and full of pride, quite right from a servant of gods!'

l. 955. δοκεῖτε δὴ, 'and you really think to dwell in your towers without sorrow!'

l. 957. Uranus and Cronus. See Introduction, p. v.

l. 960. ὑποπτήσσειν, cp. l. 29.

l. 961. γε in its common sense of 'least.' 'I am a long way at least from that, ay, all the way that is.' Cp. such phrases as ἤ τι ἢ οὐδέν, 'a very little if not nothing at all.'

l. 962. κέλευθον and ἥνπερ, cognate accusatives.

l. 964. 'Remember that it was by like acts of self-will that you got into your present troubles.'

l. 965. καθώρμισας. Nautical metaphor. See on l. 84.

l. 966. 'Trouble or not, I would rather be myself than be what you are.'

l. 968. 'For 'tis better, as I think, to serve this rock, than to be a true-born, trusty messenger to Father Zeus ;' i. e. 'my λατρεία is better than yours.' φῦναι, sarcastic. But see Appendix B.

l. 970. 'If that be insolence, it is only what those must expect who insult others.' He excuses his cutting words.

l. 971. χλιδᾶν, 'to exult in.' ἐπὶ with the dative is also found after this verb.

l. 972. 'Well, if this be exultation, may such exultation be the portion of my enemies!' Cp. l. 864.

l. 974. ξυμφοραῖς, 'on account of your misfortunes,' instrumental dative.

l. 976. Cp. l. 438, etc.

l. 977. 'From what I hear, your madness is no light attack.' νόσον, cognate accusative after μεμηνότα.

l. 978. εἰ νόσημα, sc. εἴη.

l. 980. τόδε . . τοῦπος, sc. ὤμοι. Contrary to Aeschylus' usual practice this line is divided between two speakers.

l. 981. 'Yes, but time may teach him many lessons, the use of that word among them.'

l. 982. καὶ μὴν, in rejoinder, 'and yet.'

l. 983. 'No, if I had learnt all time has to teach in the way of prudence, I should not at this moment be wasting words on a mere servant like you.'

l. 985. 'And yet *if* I *owed* him a favour, I would be ready to pay it.' γε emphasises ὀφείλων.

l. 987. Taking up the idea of l. 985, Prometheus tells Hermes that he, on his part, is even sillier than a child, if he expects to learn anything from one who owes Zeus no favours.

l. 991. πρὶν ἄν. See on l. 165.

l. 992. πρὸς ταῦτα, 'therefore,' 'in the face of this defiance.' Cp. l. 915.

l. 995. ὥστε καὶ φράσαι, 'as to go on to say,' etc.

l. 996. πρὸς οὖ. Cp. l. 761.

l. 997. ταῦτα, 'your present conduct.'

l. 998. Compare his language at l. 101.

l. 999. τόλμησον, 'take heart to,' 'make up your mind to.' Cp. l. 16. ποτε, 'at last' (*aliquando*).

l. 1000. 'In view of your present woes.' Cp. πρὸς ταῦτα above.

l. 1002. κῦμ' ὅπως παρηγορῶν, 'as though you should try to talk over a wave.' Cp. Eur. Med. 28, ὡς δὲ πέτρος ἢ θαλάσσιος κλύδων ἀκούει: also Horace, Odes, 3. 7. 21, 'Scopulis surdior Icari.'

l. 1003. 'Let it never occur to thee that,' etc. For μὴ with aorist imperative cp. l. 332.

l. 1004. 'Thy greatly hated foe,' i.e. Zeus.

l. 1005. This line is characteristic of Aeschylus. Cp. Agam. 920. The Greeks had a horror of the gestures which barbarians used so largely.

l. 1006. τοῦ παντὸς δέω, cp. l. 961.

l. 1007. 'For all the words which I speak, I seem likely to speak them all (lit. even) to no purpose.'

l. 1009. 'Like a newly-bitted colt who has (aorist participle) taken the bit between his teeth.'

l. 1010. Not yet φιλήνιος (l. 465).

l. 1011. γε emphasises the word before it, much as in l. 268. 'You rely upon a device, but know that it is an impotent one.'

l. 1013. οὐδένος μεῖον, 'less than nothing.' Cp. l. 938.

l. 1014. σκέψαι, 'consider for yourself.'

l. 1015. τρικυμία, 'a mighty wave,' each third wave being by the Greeks considered as greater than the two preceding. Cp. Latin 'fluctus decumanus.' For the general metaphor see on l. 746.

l. 1016. 'First this rugged gully shall be shattered, and thy frame shall be covered by the ruins, in the midst of which a mere ledge (lit. arm) of rock shall bear thee up.'

l. 1021. τοι, emphatic. Cp. l. 8.

l. 1022. A dog, but a winged one, and therefore not a *real* dog; see on l. 803. Eagles are called 'winged hounds' in Agam. 136. δαφοινὸς, 'ravening.'

l. 1023. 'Shall tear thy body in mighty rents.'

l. 1024. 'The eagle shall be a guest, but one who is not bidden, and one who stays all day.' See above on l. 1022, and for the particular metaphor Agam. 731.

l. 1025. κελαινόβρωτον, 'black from being gnawed.'

l. 1027. πρὶν ἄν, see on l. 165. διάδοχος, a 'successor,' 'substitute.' Cp. l. 464. See Introduction, p. xvi.

l. 1030. πρὸς ταῦτα, 'therefore.' Cp. l. 915.

l. 1031. καὶ λίαν, sc. ἀληθῶς.

l. 1034. Cp. l. 334.

l. 1036. Hermes has now exhausted all his powers of persuasion, and, though still speaking in the tone of authority, has really done his best to persuade Prometheus to abate his obstinacy. He has made a favourable impression on the Chorus, who now speak for the first time since his appearance.

l. 1036. οὐκ ἄκαιρα, 'much to the purpose.'

l. 1037. A summary of Hermes' argument, much in the same words with which he ended.

l. 1038. 'The wiser course of prudence.' The article is used because this wise course is opposed to the opposite one of αὐθαδία, as though a choice must be made between them. See on l. 778.

l. 1039. An 'argumentum ad hominem.' 'To a wise man like you it is nothing short of a disgrace to blunder.'

l. 1040. 'I well knew all the message which he proclaimed so loudly.' For the construction see on l. 23. For ἐθώϋξεν cp. l. 73. The word shows temper. Cp. ὀχλεῖς, l. 1001.

l. 1041. 'That enemy should fare badly at the hands of enemy is nothing unreasonable.' Prometheus shows himself throughout a 'good hater.' Cp. ll. 972, 978, etc.

l. 1043. πρὸς ταῦτ'. Cp. l. 915.

l. 1045. βόστρυχος, 'the wreathing flame of fire.' ἀμφήκης, 'two-edged, jagged (of lightning):' the whole phrase is a bold one.

l. 1046. 'The convulsion of angry winds.' Cp. l. 877.

l. 1047. αὐταῖς ῥίζαις, 'roots and all.' See on l. 221.

l. 1048. Observe the optatives. From the mood of mere defiance he has passed to an actual wish that the great struggle of the elements may begin, 'Oh, that the wind might shake,' etc.!

l. 1049. The subject to ξυγχώσειεν is τὸ πνεῦμα.

l. 1052. 'In the stern whirlpools of Necessity.' See on l. 514.

l. 1053. 'Do what he will he will never bring me at least to death,' (because Prometheus was immortal.) ἐμέ γε, i.e. whatever he may do to his creatures such as men.

l. 1054. 'But these are the ravings which you may hear from mad-men.' This is addressed to the Chorus, to whom Hermes now addresses himself in persuasion.

l. 1056. 'For what is his case short of actual raving?' For the negative cp. l. 248.

l. 1057. τί χαλᾷ μανιῶν; 'In what does he abate his frenzy?' For the verb cp. l. 58, and l. 256. It seems to be intransitive in the latter passage, and here.

l. 1058. 'But do you at any rate.' Cp. l. 1070.

l. 1060. I.e. μεταχωρεῖτέ ποι, 'go away, anywhere you please.'

l. 1061. μή, i.e. ἵνα μή. So often in cautions.

l. 1062. ἀτέραμνον. Cp. l. 190.

l. 1063. The Chorus indignantly reject the counsels of Hermes. 'Choose some other kind of speech and exhortation (if you must needs exhort me)—some kind by which you will persuade me!' Cp. l. 522, ἄλλου λόγου μέμνησθε.

l. 1064. 'For methinks this which thou hast dragged in out of place is wholly unbearable.'

l. 1067. The Chorus express their unshaken resolve to stand by Prometheus.

l. 1069. νόσος, cp. l. 685.

l. 1070. τῆσδ', i.e. προδοσίας. There is possibly an allusion to con-temporary events in this denunciation of treason. ἀπέπτυσα. The verb is chiefly used in this tense. Cp. Agam. 1192. Here the aorist is used of an habitual act, 'I loathe.'

l. 1071. ἀλλ' οὖν. Cp. l. 1058. 'At least remember what I tell you beforehand, and do not when caught in the toils of calamity, blame fortune.'

l. 1076. 'Do not, I adjure you, but (blame) your own selves.'

l. 1078. For ἀπέραντον cp. l. 153; for the Net of Ate (Calamity) see Agam. 360 and 1382.

l. 1080. Prometheus himself takes up the word, and announces the coming of the crash for which he had yearned (l. 1048).   καὶ μὴν, often used by dramatists where a new person comes on the stage, and here to announce this great new phase in the strife between Prometheus and Zeus. For other uses of καὶ μὴν cp. l. 246, l. 982.

l. 1082. 'The echoing thunder from the depth bellows.'

l. 1085. 'The whirlwinds roll up dust' (as though before some mighty thunderstorm).

l. 1086. As though the winds were fighting, each against each, and all against all.

l. 1089. 'In such wise (i.e. as to cause these convulsions, cp. l. 96) comes the stroke of Zeus passing manifestly towards me, to spread terror.'   φόβον τεύχουσα, not 'frightening me,' but 'intended to create terror' (present participle).

l. 1091. μητρὸς ἐμῆς. Here apparently Earth, but see on l. 210.

l. 1092. 'Air, who dost roll around for all alike the gift of light.' With the last line of this appeal, and with its language throughout, should be compared the first utterance of Prometheus (ll. 88–113). See Introduction, p. vii.

APPENDIX.

A.

List of passages in which the text of this edition differs from that of Dindorf's Second Edition, (Oxford, 1851.)

l. 2. ἄβατον. Dindorf, from quotations of Aeschylus found in old writers, reads ἄβροτον. If Aeschylus wrote this, he had probably mis-understood the phrase νὺξ ἀβρότη in Homer, as though the adjective meant ἀπάνθρωπος (cp. l. 20).

l. 17. ἐξωριάζειν. D. has εὐωριάζειν, a word which is found elsewhere, and which contrasts well in sense with βαρύ.

l. 38. This line is probably, as suggested by a friendly critic, an interpolation; being weak in itself, and spoiling the symmetry of a dialogue otherwise composed of speeches of two lines and one alternately.

l. 49. ἐπαχθῆ. D. has ἐπράχθη, which is the reading of the MSS. If retained, it must be taken: 'All things have been attained, except to rule over the gods.' But this should rather be πέπρακται, and the sense is not good in any case. ἐπαχθῆ is an old conjecture (Stanley's) which has been received into many texts. Elmsley (Ed. Rev.) objects that ἀχθεινὺς, not ἐπαχθὴς, is the tragic word.

l. 59. πόρους. D. has πόρον.

l. 87. τέχνης. D. has τύχης, which is perhaps easier.

l. 181. διατόρος. D. has διάτορος.

l. 248. D. has θνητούς γ' ἔπαυσα, κ. τ. λ.

l. 350. ὤμοις. D. has ὤμοιν.

l. 371. D. reads θερμοῖς ἀπλάτου, κ.τ.λ.

l. 426. ἀδαμαντοδέτοις. D. has ἀκαμαντοδέτοις, which is the word in the MSS.

l. 427. Ἄτλανθ'. D. has Ἄτλαν.

l. 430. ὑποστενάζει. D. has ὀχῶν στενάζει.

l. 568. ἄλευε δᾶ. D. has ἄλευ δᾶ.

l. 735. Ἀσιάδ'. D. has Ἀσιδ'.

l. 770. D. has οὐ δῆτα, πλὴν ἐὰν ἐγὼ 'κ δεσμῶν λυθῶ.

l. 850. D. has ἐπώνυμον δὲ τῶν Διὸς γέννημ' ἀφῶν, and places the preceding line in square brackets.

B.

The following passages deserve a special notice, both from their intrinsic interest, and because they illustrate the same principles of criticism.

ll. 255–8. It has been proposed (by Welcker) to distribute these lines as follows :—

XO. τοιοῖσδε δή σε Ζεὺς ἐπ' αἰτιάμασιν—
ΠΡ. αἰκίζεταί τε κοὐδαμῆ χαλᾷ κακῶν,
XO. οὐδ' ἔστιν ἄθλου τέρμα σοι προκείμενον ;
ΠΡ. οὐκ ἄλλο γ' οὐδὲν πλὴν ὕταν κείνῳ δοκῇ.

By this arrangement symmetry and spirit are restored to the dialogue. It may be observed that in the principal MS. of Aeschylus a change of speaker is usually only marked by a line drawn at the side, which may easily have been omitted sometimes, though cases where this has manifestly taken place are not numerous.

ll. 968–970. 'Almost equally plausible is the (Hermann's) redistribution of Prom. 972–3 (968–9) κρεῖσσον γὰρ οἶμαι κ.τ.λ., assigning those lines to Hermes, not to Prometheus—a notion which would be improved by adopting Mr. Paley's independent suggestion, that οἶμαι is to be taken parenthetically. Yet it may be answered, and we think with force, that while the new arrangement suits the first of the two verses equally well with the old, it is less appropriate to the second, the language of which can hardly be other than ironical, and therefore is not very likely to be applied by Hermes to his own position. Either disposition makes one of the speakers accept the taunt implied in the words of the other; but while Prometheus might dwell, even with pride, on his servitude to the rock, Hermes would hardly talk of himself as born the trusty messenger of Zeus, especially as his *birth* to service, which, under such circumstances, could only be mentioned contemptuously, had not been alluded to by his enemy. The following lines too seem to us decidedly to negative Hermann's view : l. 974 (970) would not be a natural answer to the supposed taunt of the younger God, which could not fairly be taken as a serious expostulation ; nor could l. 975 (971) be referred back to ll. 970–1 (966–7), separated as they are by two intervening speeches, even if its language did not clearly point out ll. 972–3 (968–9), as those to which it is intended to apply.'

From a review of Hermann's Aeschylus by Professor Conington. *Edinburgh Review,* 1854.

C.

Another view as to the geography of the wanderings of Io is put forward by Mr. Douglas W. Freshfield in a letter to 'The Academy' dated June 21, 1879.

After discussing the difficulties of l. 420, and proposing to read (with Boissonade) 'Αβαρίας, i. e. the land of the Avars, Mr. Freshfield continues :—

'Again in l. 735 the

$$\text{ὑβριστὴν ποταμὸν οὐ ψευδώνυμον}$$

is assumed to be the Araxes, and in consequence Aeschylus is said to have confused that river and the Kouban. Was not κόραξ also a word of insult? A river of this name—the modern Bsyb, flowing into the sea at Pitzonuda—was the ancient boundary of Colchis. It is one of the largest rivers on the coast, and often forces modern travellers to go up some way into the mountains before they can find a way southwards.

If Aeschylus referred to this river, the whole passage is a singularly accurate sketch of the journey along the Circassian coast.'

The subject is further treated in letters which appeared in the same journal on July 12, July 19, and August 9 of the same year.

THE END.

www.ingramcontent.com/pod-product-compliance
Lightning Source LLC
Chambersburg PA
CBHW020803020726
47495CB00008B/2571